# COLD SKIN

Albert Sánchez Piñol was born in Barcelona in 1965. He is an anthropologist, non-fiction writer and novelist writing in Catalan and Castilian Spanish. His first novel, *Cold Skin* has been translated into thirty-seven languages, won the Ojo Critico Narrativa prize on its original publication in Catalan in 2003 and is being adapted for film. He is also the author of *Pandora in the Congo*, among other books.

# COLD SKIN

## ALBERT SÁNCHEZ PIÑOL

CANONGATE
*Edinburgh · London*

This Canons edition published by Canongate Books in 2016

First published in Great Britain in 2006 by
Canongate Books Ltd, 14 High Street,
Edinburgh EH1 1TE

www.canongate.tv

Originally published in Spain in 2002 under the title *La Pell Freda* by La Campana.
This English translation published by arrangement with Farrar,
Straus and Giroux L.L.C., 19 Union Square West, New York, NY 10003, USA.
All rights reserved.

1

This work was published with a grant from the General Books Council for
the Archives and Libraries of the Spanish Ministry of Culture

*British Library Cataloguing-in-Publication Data*
A catalogue record for this book is available on
request from the British Library

ISBN 978 1 78211 717 9

Typeset in Van Dijck by Palimpsest Book Production Ltd,
Grangemouth, Stirlingshire

Printed and bound in Great Britain by Clays Ltd, St Ives plc

# 1

We are never very far from those we hate. For this very reason, we shall never be truly close to those we love. An appalling fact, I knew it well enough when I embarked. But some truths deserve our attention; others are best left alone.

We had our first sighting of the island at dawn. It had been thirty-three days since the dolphins fell away sternward and nineteen since the crew's breath first expelled clouds of vapour. The Scottish sailors protected themselves with gloves that reached up to their elbows. Their furs were so heavy that the men resembled walruses. Those frigid latitudes were torture for the Senegalese. The captain allowed them to use potato grease as a protective coating on their cheeks and forehead. The substance would run and trickle into their eyes. It brought tears but they never complained.

"Look, on the horizon. Your island," the captain said to me.

I could not make it out. I saw only that same cold ocean, sealed off by distant clouds. We were quite far south, but neither the silhouettes nor the perils of Antarctic icebergs had enlivened our crossing. Not a single ice mountain, no trace even of those raw, spectacular and melting giants. Against the privations of the south we struggled, but it denied us its majesty. My fate, then, was to stand on the threshold of a border I would never cross. The captain passed me his binoculars. And now? Do you see it? Yes, I saw it. A sliver of land crushed between the greys of the ocean and sky, encircled by a necklace of white foam. And that was all. I had to wait another hour yet, and then, as we drew nearer, the outlines of the island grew visible to the naked eye.

Here was my future abode: an L-shaped expanse that measured barely a mile from end to end. At the northern extreme stood a solid rock elevation crowned by a lighthouse. The tower was imposing not so much for its size as for the island's reduced dimensions, which gave it, in contrast, the solidity of a megalith. At the bend in the L, on a small rise to the south, was the weather official's cottage. Or rather, mine. The two structures were united by a sort of narrow valley overrun with damp undergrowth. The trees grew like a herd of huddled animals seeking their own kind. Moss protected them, a moss more compact than garden hedge and knee high. It stained the tree trunks like a three-coloured blight – blue, violet and black, an unusual phenomenon.

The island was ringed round with small reefs, scattered here and there. They made it impossible to weigh anchor any closer than one thousand feet from the island's only beach, which spread out in front of the house. I had no choice but to haul my body and baggage into a dinghy. It had to be taken as an act of kindness that the captain accompanied me onto dry land. Nothing obliged him. But during the journey we had come to one of those understandings that sometimes arise between men of different generations. He grew up near the docks of Hamburg and later moved to Denmark. If there was anything remarkable about him, it was his eyes. The rest of the world fell away when he looked at someone. He scrutinised others with the shrewdness of an entomologist and every situation with the finesse of an expert. Some would have mistaken this for severity. I believe that it was his way of expressing the benevolence he hid in the recesses of his soul. He would never confess this love for his fellow man, but it was evident in all his actions. The captain always treated me with the courtesy of an executioner. If he could do anything for me, he would. After all, who was I? A man closer to youth than maturity, heading toward a tiny island swept by harsh polar winds. I would have to live, in a solitude like exile, for twelve months, far from civilisation, with a job as monotonous as it was insignificant: to log the intensity, direction and frequency of the winds. That was how the international marine accords defined my assignment. Naturally, the pay was good. But no one accepts such a fate for money.

Four dinghies were enough to carry the captain, twenty

sailors and me onto the beach. It would take the men a while to unload a whole year's worth of provisions, not to mention the trunks and personal effects I'd brought with me. Stacks of books. I knew I would have time on my hands and wanted to delve into the reading that had been denied to me in the past.

"Well, let's get going," said the captain when he realised that it would be a slow job.

So he and I trudged along the sand. A steep path led up to the house. The prior tenant had taken pains to put up a railing. Driftwood polished by the ocean, crudely nailed. It was obviously the work of a rational mind. And as incredible as it may seem, that was the first clue that started me thinking about the man I was meant to replace. That individual was an actual person and I was witnessing an effect he had had on the world, gratuitous as it seemed. I thought about him and said out loud, "It's strange the weather official hasn't come out to meet us. You'd think he'd be well pleased that he's being replaced."

As often happened with the captain, I spoke, only to bite my tongue a second afterward. His thoughts raced ahead of mine. The house was in front of us. A conical roof, with slate shingles and red brick walls. The building lacked both grace and harmony. In the Alps, it would have been a mountain refuge, a retreat in the woods or a customs booth.

The captain inspected the scene, without moving, like someone sniffing out danger. I had given the initiative over to him. An early morning wind moved the branches of the four trees that marked the corners of the house. They looked like Canadian oaks. The air wasn't freezing, but it was uncomfortable. An eerie sense of desolation pervaded everything, but its nature was hard to grasp. The problem wasn't so much what was there as what was missing. Where was the weather official? Was he off completing some task of his station? Or simply going for a walk around the island? Gradually, I began to notice ominous signs. The windows were small rectangles of thick glass. The wooden shutters hung open, banging. It jarred me. Around the walls of the house, you could still make out the remains of an abandoned garden. Its borders were traced by half-buried stones. But most of the plants were crushed, as though they had been trampled on by a herd of elephants.

The captain made one of his characteristic gestures: chin up, as if the collar of his blue overcoat were just slightly asphyxiating. Then he pushed the door, which opened with the creak of a profaned Egyptian tomb. If doors could talk, that screech said, Enter at your own risk. Thus, we entered.

The sight was straight out of the diary of an African explorer. It was as if a column of tropical ants had overrun the space, devouring all life. The basic furnishings were essentially intact. More than destruction; abandonment. The space was one open room. The bed, fireplace and the stacked firewood were all in place. The table had fallen over.

The mercury barometer was in one piece. The kitchen utensils were gone – I don't know why, but this detail struck me as an inscrutable mystery. My predecessor's personal effects and equipment were nowhere to be seen. But the neglect seemed to me more the product of some strange madness than that of a natural catastrophe. The scene was grim, but overall the house was still habitable. We could hear the murmur of the waves distinctly.

"Where should we leave the senior official of air and wind's belongings?" asked Sow, one of the Senegalese, as he came in. The sailors had been able to lug the baggage up from the beach.

"Here, anywhere, somewhere inside, it's all the same," I said roughly, in order to cover up the shock the unexpected voice had given me.

The captain took out his disgust about the situation on the sailor. "Come on, Sow; get the boys to clean up this mess."

While the men went to work unloading the trunks and putting things in order, the captain suggested we go to the lighthouse.

"Maybe we'll find your predecessor," he said when the sailors could no longer hear us.

As far as the captain knew, the lighthouse was also inhabited. He couldn't remember exactly who it was, the Dutch or the French, but it belonged to somebody. After all, the lighthouse keeper was the weather official's neighbour. It seemed logical and fitting that they would at least have struck up a passing friendship. We talked of finding the weather official, but we couldn't account for the house's condition. No matter what, it was time to go to the lighthouse.

I still recall the uneasiness I felt on that short walk. The forest was unlike any we had seen before. A path beaten down by men's footsteps led us on an almost direct route to the lighthouse. It deviated only where the treacherous moss hid pockets of mud and black ooze. The ocean, just behind the trees, grazed us with its soft cadence. The worst of it was, precisely, the silence. Or rather, the noiselessness. The melodies associated with forest wildlife were absent. We heard no birds or chirping insects. Many large tree trunks had grown twisted by the wind's force. From the boat, the forest had looked extremely thick. Distance is often misleading when it comes to density, whether it is human or vegetable. Not this time. The trees grew so close together that it was often difficult to tell whether two sprang from the same root or whether they were separate. A series of narrow streams broke up our path. One broad step was enough to ford them.

The lighthouse tower appeared suddenly, rising behind the tallest trees. The path ended at the edge of the forest. We could see the pedestal of raw stone on which the structure had been built. It was enveloped by the ocean on three sides. The waves must have pounded violently against the rock when the sea was rough. But whoever the architect was, he had done a thorough job. A rounded and compact surface to withstand the ocean's violence, five well-placed windows, a narrow balcony with a rusty railing, a pointed light tower. The purpose of the balcony was completely incomprehensible. Sticks and crossed posts, often with their points sharpened. Was it scaffolding for repair work? We had neither the leisure nor the strength to wonder.

"Hello! Anybody there? Hello!" called the captain, striking the steel door with the palm of his hand. There was no answer, but that impulse was enough to discover that the door wasn't locked. It was extremely solid. The iron was inches thick and reinforced by dozens of lead rivets. It was so bulky that it took the two of us to shove it open. The lighting inside was uncanny. The sun that filtered through created cathedral-like effects. An incipient coating of lime scattered its whiteness across the concave walls. The stairs rose in a spiral that clung to the rock. As far as we could see, that lower space was used as a storage room, with a large quantity of staples and reserves.

The captain muttered something under his breath that I couldn't make out. He began to climb the stairs with determination. The ninety-six steps ended on a wooden platform that served as a floor to the space above. A push up to the trapdoor and we were inside.

In fact, it was a perfectly ordered and snug dwelling. An elbow-shaped stove was located in the centre of the almost circular space. A wall with a door broke up the room's roundness. The kitchen was most likely to be found back there. More stairs led to another floor that surely held the lighthouse's lamp. These things seemed all in order. What didn't make sense was the disposition of the objects.

Everything had been oddly arranged on the floor, all along the walls. Objects that would normally be placed on tables or shelves were aligned on the ground. And every crate had something to weigh it down, whether it had a top or not. For example: a shoe box, and over the shoes, a coal iron. An oil drum: a foot-and-a-half tall cylinder filled with dirty clothes. A scrap of wood on top compressed the pieces of clothing. Both the iron and the piece of wood were insufficient covers. In any case, they did nothing to hide the stench, if that was their intended effect. It was as though the owner had worried that the contents would escape like birds if freed from the laws of gravity and had reinforced these small containers with heavy counterweights.

Finally, the bed. It was an old thing, with a headboard of thin iron bars. And, covered in three thick blankets, there was a man.

We had obviously surprised him. His eyes were wide open when we came in. But he didn't move. The blankets went up to his nose and covered him like a bear's skin. He looked defenceless, forlorn and ferocious at the same time. Under the bed, there was a chamber pot filled to the rim with urine.

"Good day, maritime signal technician. We're replacing your neighbour, the weather official," the captain said without mincing words and pointing in the direction of the house. "Do you know where he is?"

The captain's words reminded me that we were a mile away from the landing beach. I suddenly felt that that distance was longer than the entire route between Europe and the island. I also remembered that the captain would be leaving, and soon.

A hand covered in black hair moved idly in the bed. But it gave up halfway through.

The captain was exasperated by the man's stillness. "Don't you understand me? You don't understand my language? Do you speak French? Dutch?"

But the man just kept gazing at him fixedly. He didn't even bother to pull the blankets away from his face.

"For God's sake!" the captain bellowed, waving his fist. "I have an important voyage to complete. And I'm in transit! I agreed to go off course by request of the International Maritime Federation in order to drop this man here and pick up his predecessor. Is that clear? But the current weather official isn't here. He isn't here. Can you please tell me where he is?"

The lighthouse keeper's eyes roved from the captain to me.

Flushing, the captain persisted. "I am a captain and it

is in my power to bring you to justice if you deny me crucial information concerning the safety of goods and crew. I repeat for the last time, where is the designated weather official for this island?"

There was an awkward silence. We had just about given up trying to communicate with this character when he threw us off guard with the accent of an Austrian artilleryman.

"I regret that I cannot answer that question."

The captain changed his tone.

"Well, that's better. Why didn't you answer me? Are you in contact with the weather official? When was the last time you saw him?"

Once again, the lighthouse keeper shut himself up in silence.

"Get up!" the captain ordered brusquely.

The man obeyed, taking his time. He threw off the covers, and pulled out his feet. He was quite solidly built. His movements were those of an uprooted tree learning to walk. The lighthouse keeper remained on the bed looking down at the ground. Naked. He wasn't ashamed to expose himself. But the captain averted his gaze, offended by a rank odour to which the lighthouse keeper seemed oblivious. The man's chest was covered in a mat of hair that twined up his shoulders like wild vines. The tangle took on a junglelike density below his navel. His member was enormous, but flaccid. It unsettled me that even this organ was covered with hair up to the foreskin. What are you looking down there for? I said to myself, and wrenched my eyes up to meet the man's face. His beard was as wild as a patriarch's. He was one of those men whose hairline begins barely an inch and a half above his eyebrows, and thickly at that. The lighthouse keeper sat on the mattress with his hands resting on his knees, arms resting side by side. His eyes and nose were squashed in the middle of his face, leaving plenty of room for a pair of wide, square cheekbones. The interrogation seemed to leave him unfazed. I could no longer tell if it was out of discipline or lethargy. But as I watched him, I noticed a tick that gave away the tension underneath: his lips opened and closed like a bat's, showing a set of widely spaced teeth. The captain stooped down until his face was an inch away from the other's ear.

"Have you gone mad? Are you aware of the implications? This is a breach of international regulations. What is your name?"

The man looked at the captain.

"Whose?"

"Yours! I'm talking to you! What is your given name?"

"Gruner. Gruner."

The captain said, pronouncing every syllable, "For the last time, Maritime Signal Technician Gruner, I beg of you, where is the weather official?"

Without meeting the captain's eyes, the man said after a hesitation, "It's impossible for me to answer that question."

"He's mad, he's obviously gone mad." The captain gave up, pacing like a caged animal. Then, as if Gruner weren't there, the captain began to rifle through his things with the air of a police inspector. I went into the neighbouring room and saw a book on the floor. It was also held down by a stone. I thumbed through it.

In an attempt to start him talking, I said, "I'm also familiar with Dr Frazer's writing, although I have no set opinions about it. I'm not sure whether *The Golden Bough* is a brilliant piece of scholarship or a magnificent diversion."

"That book isn't mine and I haven't read it."

It was a strange sort of logic. He said it as though there was some kind of connection between owning and reading a book. In any case, nothing more was said. Without even taking his hands off his knees, he gave me a dejected look.

"Oh, leave him be," the captain broke in, having failed to discover anything of interest. "This one hasn't even read his codebook. He puts me on edge."

All we could do was to go back to the weather official's house. But halfway there, while still in the forest, the captain grabbed my sleeve, stopping me short.

"The nearest landmass is Bouvet Island, claimed by the Norwegians, six hundred leagues southwest of here." And after a long and considered pause, "Are you certain you want to stay? I don't like it. This is just a chunk of rock, lost in the middle of the least trafficked ocean on the planet, at the same latitude as the deserts of Patagonia. I could convince any administrative commission that this site doesn't fulfill the most basic requirements. No one would hold it against you. You have my word."

Should I turn back? I think it was the absurdity of the question that made up my mind. I hadn't travelled halfway around the world only to turn around when I got there.

"The weather official's cottage is in good condition, I have a year's worth of provisions and nothing to stop me from fulfilling my duties. For the rest, my predecessor was most likely the victim of some stupid and fatal accident. Maybe suicide, who knows. But I don't think that this man Gruner is responsible. In my opinion, he is a danger only to himself. The solitude has got to him, and he must fear that we shall blame him for his colleague's disappearance. That would explain his behaviour."

As I said this, I was surprised by how plausible it all sounded. I had only left out my feeling of foreboding. The captain gazed at me with the eyes of a cobra. His body swayed slightly, weight shifting from one foot to the other, his hands beneath the jacket.

"Don't worry about me," I insisted.

"Some disillusionment has brought you here, I'm sure of it," he stated with conviction.

After deliberating, I said, "Who knows."

"No," he answered, "it's obvious. You've come here out of spite." He spread his arms wide like a magician proving his innocence, or a gambler folding his hand. His gesture said: There's nothing more I can do for you.

We had come down to the beach. The twenty sailors longed for the order to return to the ship. For no apparent reason, they were restless with impatience. The Senegalese, Sow, gave me a reassuring slap on the back. The black man was completely bald and had a bright white beard.

He winked and said, "Pay no attention to the boys. They're young sailors, new recruits from the Scottish Highlands. A cactus in the Yucatán understands the mysteries and lore of the sea better than them. They're not even white; they're red. And everybody knows that Scots are superstitious, prey to tavern gossip. Eat well, work hard, and keep looking in the mirror to remember what you look like. Talk to yourself so you don't lose the habit of speech, and keep your mind busy with simple tasks. What is one year of our lives worth compared to the patience of the Good Lord?"

Then they got into the dinghies and grabbed the oars. The sailors looked at me with a mixture of compassion and confusion. They gazed like children seeing an ostrich for the first time, or like peaceful citizens facing a cartload of wounded returning from war. The ship sailed away, with the sluggishness of a wheelbarrow. I kept my eyes on it until it was just a dot on the horizon. I felt a sense of irreparable loss in the instant that that dot was blotted out, a kind of steel ring pressing in on my skull. I couldn't tell whether it arose from a longing for civilisation, a prisoner's panic, or simply fear.

I lingered awhile longer on the beach. As for the inlet, it was a precise half-moon shape. Volcanic rocks jutted out on the left and right; jagged stones, covered in sharp edges, perforated like cheese. The sand was the texture of incense ash, grey and compressed. Small round holes gave away the hiding places of crustaceans. The rocks made the waves break half dead on the shore; a thin film of white foam traced the boundary between earth and sky. The undertow had driven dozens of cleanly polished tree trunks onto the coastline. Some were the roots of old trees that had been chopped down. The tides had formed them with an artist's precision, leaving sculptures of a rare and contorted beauty. The sky was tinged a gloomy shade of tarnished silver, with the even darker tones of a rusty suit of armour. The sun was no more than an orange suspended halfway up, small and continuously covered by clouds that grudgingly filtered the light. A sun that, because of its latitude, would never reach its zenith. My description isn't trustworthy. It is what I saw. But the landscape we see beyond our eyes tends to be a reflection of what we hide, within us.

# 2

There are times when we must bargain for our future with the past. You sit on a lonely rock and try to negotiate between the devastating failures that came before and utter darkness that is on its way. In that sense, I trusted that the passage of time, contemplation and distance would work miracles. Nothing less would have brought me to that island.

I spent the rest of that unreal morning unpacking, classifying and putting my belongings in order with the mind-set of a laical monk. What was my life on the island to be but that of a fact-collecting hermit? Most of the books fitted on the shelves that I inherited from my colleague, but those planks told me nothing new about him. Next were the flour sacks, tins, salted meat, the capsules of ether for unexpected pain and thousands of vitamin C tablets, indispensable against scurvy. The instruments of measurement – thermometers, two mercury barometers, three diachronic modulators and the very complete first aid kit – were all, fortunately, intact. I will have to draw from the resources of science in order to describe the curiosities that I found in trunk 22-E, where the letters and petitions were kept.

Taking advantage of my stay in such an inhospitable place, Russian researchers from Kiev University had asked me to conduct a biological experiment. For reasons that I never fully understood, the island's geographic placement was ideal for the proliferation of small rodents. They proposed that I breed a species of long-haired dwarf rabbits from Siberia, especially suited to the climate. If the project was a success, passing ships would find a supply of fresh meat. They had left me two heavily illustrated books on the subject that gave instructions on how to care for the woolly rabbits. But I didn't have a single cage or rabbit, long-haired or otherwise. I remembered, however, the little laugh of the ship's cook each time the captain and I congratulated him on those stews that were listed on the menu as "Russian rabbit in Kiev sauce".

The Geographical Society of Berlin had sent fifteen jars filled with formaldehyde. According to the instructions they entrusted me with, if I would be so kind, fill them with "interesting autochthonous insects, providing that they are classified as *Hydrometridae Halobates* or *Chironomidae Pontomyia*, which are not averse to water". With typical German efficiency, the notebook had been protected in waterproof silk. In case my skills as a polyglot weren't sufficient, the instructions were translated into eight languages including Finnish and Turkish. It informed me in severe Gothic lettering that the jars of formaldehyde were the property of the Republic of Germany and that "partial damage or total breakage of one or more jars" would lead to a corresponding administrative sanction. To my great relief, a last-minute addendum informed me that my status as scientific researcher absolved me from those sanctions. What lenience! Unfortunately, it didn't mention what the *Hydrometridae Halobates* or the *Chironomidae Pontomyia* looked like, whether they were butterflies or beetles, or who might care about them and why.

A company from Lyon, associated with a merchant shipping outfit, requested my services in the field of mineralogy. Their petition came with a small instrument for research analysis and its instruction manual. In the event that I discovered deposits of gold at least 60 per cent pure, and only under those circumstances, they would be obliged if I would inform them "with the maximum speed and urgency". Of course, if I found a gold mine, it goes without saying that my first reaction would be to go running over to some offices in Lyon so they could lay claim to it. Finally, expressing himself in an ornate hand, a Catholic missionary asked that I fill in "with the care and patience of a saint" some questionnaires with which to quiz the local indigenous people. "Don't be discouraged if the Bantu chiefs of the island are very shy," he advised. "Preach by example and kneel as you recite the rosary. That will inspire them to follow the path of faith." The missionary was no doubt deeply misinformed as to my destination, where it would be difficult to find a Bantu kingdom, let alone a republic. Just when only two crates were left unopened, that unexpected envelope appeared: the letter.

I'd like to say that I ripped it up without reading it. I couldn't. Days later, I would go over what happened next. And why? Because that blasted letter angered me so much that I forgot all about the two sealed crates. I didn't examine their contents, and soon after, that almost got me killed.

The letter was from one of my old cohorts. It was militancy that had brought me to the island in the first place. Or should I say the falling-out with a cause. The world had never seen such a noble and selfless struggle. That is, until we were victorious. From that moment on, my comrades set to turning the tide of persecution. That was all. The only difference between the new government and our enemies was the colours in the flag. It just went to show that humanity was caught up in a series of invisible gears, destined to turn forever on themselves. One could argue that it was not I who had abandoned the cause, but the cause that had abandoned me. That was why I had chosen to flee from the world of men.

What infuriated me most was that the letter said absolutely nothing. Without being impertinent, its authors had made quite sure that no shred of truth should appear in those lines. They gave me nothing to reproach them for, not realising that this was the most hateful stance of all. Far worse was the insistent and subtle way that they asked for my silence. All they were concerned about was that I might continue on with the same work as I had in the past, but for the enemy. They kept up the same sham about how much they regretted my desertion, even offering to take me back should I decide to return home. They truly believed that my bitterness was born out of personal ambition. More than a letter, it was a catalogue of pettiness. Yes, I insulted them by placing over a thousand leagues between us. But I was no fool. In the midst of my fury, I did not curse those people, just the sentiments that still chained me to the past. I was a recluse not on the island, but in my memory.

# 3

With only two crates remaining, I sank down on a wooden stool like someone who has gone a great distance. What could I do? I thought it would be a good idea to go back to the lighthouse. If I couldn't make peace with its keeper, I would at least clear my head. It could be that Gruner's insanity was merely transitory. I was willing to forgive him for it. After all, the captain hadn't hesitated to burst into his home with all the subtlety of a crowing rooster. And we had woken him up. A responsible lighthouse keeper sleeps during the day and works at night, keeping the beam steady. The captain and I were immune to the constant and almost obscene human contact of life on a boat. Not him. Imagine the shock of seeing two strangers there, at the end of the world.

The island's vitality was concentrated in the forest. But the deeper I went into the thick of it, the more I associated it with life in its latency; accidental, fearful and wild. Thick and seemingly solid branches stuck out of the undergrowth. Bend them, and they broke like carrots. Soon, winter would come and snow would beat down the trees with hammer blows. That forest reminded me of an army that surrenders before the battle. But halfway there, I stopped in front of a large marble plaque with a bare bronze pipe sticking out of it. The plaque was set into the face of solid rock, framed by black moss. It was a good place for it, because for lack of any other elevation, that plaque formed the centre of a small watery shell. A continuous stream of water flowed out of the pipe. The rivulet poured into a big iron bucket, spilling over its borders. Another empty one was waiting by its side. I realised that this was the spring that belonged to the lighthouse.

It's strange the way we edit our perceptions. I hadn't noticed the fountain when the captain and I first walked by. We hadn't seen it because we were concentrating on more important things. But now that I was alone, completely alone, a bronze pipe vomiting up water was of vital interest. I went closer and saw an inscription scrawled over the pipe. It said:

*Gruner lives here*
*Gruner made this fountain*
*Gruner wrote this*
*Gruner knows how to defend himself*
*Gruner rules the waves*
*Gruner has what he wants and wants only what he has*
*Gruner is Gruner and Gruner is Gruner*
*Dix it et fecit*

It was a blow. I could forget about any possibility of companionship. That slab exposed a mind as fractured as it was lost. But I had nothing better to do than continue on to the lighthouse. The door was closed when I got to the building. I called out, in imitation of the captain.

No one answered; the only sound was of the waves washing against the rocks nearby. "Gruner! Gruner!" Cupping my hands around my mouth, "Gruner, Gruner! Hello there, Gruner! Please, open up. I'm the weather official!"

No answer. The balcony was some twenty feet above the door. I gazed up at it, hoping his shape would appear. I noticed that shards of wood had been attached to the balcony's base. The first time I saw it, I had assumed it was some sort of crude scaffolding. I was wrong. It was different in shape from the original iron supports that held the balcony to the wall. They were sharp, pointed stakes. Actually, the entire balcony was enveloped in the structure, giving it the look of a makeshift hedgehog. I could hear the sound of tinkling as the wind blew. Close to the ground, the lighthouse's walls were plastered with broad nails, hung with string. Empty cans, some in pairs, dangled off the strings. The wind tousled them against each other and the walls, just like cowbells. There were even more bewildering particulars: the cracks between the stones swarmed with nails, their points sticking out. Nails and broken glass; all sorts of glass. The sun made them sparkle in varied tones of red and green. The coating of nails and glass ended a little higher up. The stones in the wall had been fused with an improvised grout, creating the seamless surface of an Incan temple. You couldn't wedge a baby's fingernail between them. I circled the lighthouse: the whole thing was protected by these ridiculous fortifications. When I got back to the door, I saw Gruner on the balcony. He was aiming a double-barrelled shotgun at me.

"Hello, Gruner. Remember me?" I said. "I'd like to talk. After all, we're neighbours. Rather curious neighbourhood, don't you think?"

"Come any closer and I'll shoot."

My experience was that you don't give prior warning when you're about to kill a man. If you do, then you aren't very serious about killing him in the first place.

"Be reasonable, Gruner," I insisted.

He didn't answer, just kept the gun trained on me from his balcony perch.

"When does your contract expire?" I asked, just to say something. "Is your replacement coming soon?"

"I'll kill you."

I shrugged my shoulders and walked slowly away. I turned after reaching the forest; he was still on the balcony, legs spread apart, with the stance of an alpine sharpshooter. Even his right eye was twisted shut.

The rest of the day was uneventful. I finished organising the house. An uncanny feeling came over me. I unconsciously bit my bottom lip until it bled. I very consciously uncorked a barrel of cognac. Half drunk, half sober and somewhat giddy, I laid the fireplace. Countless poets have written about homesickness. I've never been able to appreciate poetry. I think that pain is a sensation more primitive than language; any attempt to articulate it is futile. And I no longer had a homeland.

My gloomy thoughts fed off the encroaching darkness. In those parts of the world, night didn't fall, it took over by force. A fright: suddenly, a flash of white light illuminated the murkiness of the house, disappearing as quickly as it came. It was the lighthouse. Gruner had lit it up; the beam began its swooping course, shining on and off through my windows. I couldn't understand it. The light hit me directly. That meant that it was angled too low to guide distant ships. What a cold fish, I thought. One could assume, for example, that he had come to the island to be alone. But we had two very different conceptions of solitude. I viewed authentic solitude as an inner state that didn't exclude a casual acquaintance between neighbours. He, on the other hand, chose to treat all humans like lepers. At any rate, Gruner's eccentricities didn't interest me very much just then.

I remember lighting the oil lamp. I sat down at the table and planned out my daily schedule. That's how it was. The fireplace was at one end; I was sitting at the desk on the other side of the building. The bed, which resembled my bunk aboard ship, and the door were to the right. On the other wall, boxes and trunks; it was all very spare. Just then, I heard a pleasing sound far off. It was more or less like a small herd of goats trotting in the distance. At first, I confused it with the pattering of rain; the sound of heavy and distinct drops. I got up and looked out of the closest window. It wasn't raining. The full moon stained the ocean's surface in a violet hue. The light bathed the driftwood lying on the beach. It was easy to imagine them as body parts; dismembered and immobile. The whole thing brought to mind a petrified forest. But it wasn't raining. I sat down again and then I saw it. It. I remember thinking that my eyes had been robbed of their reason.

The lower part of the door had a kind of a hatch. A round hole covered by a movable flap. The arm was sticking out of it. A whole arm naked and elongated. It was feeling around for something inside with spastic jerks. Maybe the lock? It was not a human arm. Although the oil lamp and the fire gave only a dim light, I could see that the three bones at the elbow were smaller and pointier than ours.

Not a speck of fat; pure muscle coated with shark skin. But the hand was worst of all. The fingers were joined by a membrane that went all the way up to the nails.

Confusion was followed by a wave of panic. I shouted in terror and jumped out of the chair at the same time. A multitude of voices answered my cry. They were everywhere. The house was surrounded by unearthly screams, something between a hippopotamus's moan and a hyena's shriek. I was so terrified that my own fear felt unreal. I looked out another window, my mind a blank.

I could sense them out there more than I could see them. They ran around the house as agile as gazelles. The full moon cut out their silhouettes. As soon as I could make one out, it fled from view. It stopped, twisting its head with the vivacity of a snake, whistling, running, going back, joining a few others, who knows why, and all at lightning speed. I heard something smash; they had broken the windowpane behind me. Only their unbridled appetite saved me. The window was a small rectangle, but it was big enough for a lithe body to get through. All the same, their eagerness drove them to try and jump inside at once, making it impossible to get through. The scene was lit up by the lighthouse's beam. That brief flash illuminated absolute horror. Six or seven tentacle-like arms waved in front of their faces that came screaming out of some amphibious underworld: eyes like eggs, pupils like needles, holes instead of noses, no eyebrows, no lips, a huge mouth.

I acted more on instinct than common sense. I grabbed a thick log from the fireplace and, with a cry, shoved it against those marauding arms. Sparks, blue blood, whimpers of pain and fragments of charred wood flew. When the last arm pulled away, I threw the log outside. The windows had storm shutters on the inside. I wanted to shut out and bar them, but the last claw seized the moment to slash at my neck. I'm still amazed that I managed to keep my wits about me. Instead of grabbing for the monster's wrists, I snatched its finger. I doubled it over until the bone snapped. I took a step back. I gathered the coals from the fire into an empty sack and threw them out the window. That deluge triggered a round of invisible moans. In the momentary calm that followed, I closed the wooden shutters as fast as I could.

There were still three windows with all their shutters hanging wide open. I flew from one window to the next, closing the wooden panels and drawing the bars across them. Somehow, the creatures understood the situation and circled the house, trying to reach into each window as it slammed shut. I could follow them by their ever more anxious howls. It was just good luck that I got to the shutters first. Their frustration when the last one closed was expressed as a long and bone-chilling scream. Ten, eleven, twelve voices were howling in unison.

They were still out there. Desperate, trying to work out what to do, I searched for some kind of weapon. The axe, I chanted to myself. But I couldn't see it and had no time to look for it so I settled for a stick. Now a mass of monsters were pounding against a window. The wood trembled but the bar was strong. And they weren't following any kind of plan; the banging went on, without order or purpose. Under those conditions, I couldn't even defend myself, only wait for who knew what. I thought again of that arm in the hatch: it was still there. That sight almost pushed me over the edge. The accumulated tension made me go straight for that horrible limb with a rage I would never have thought myself capable of. I pummeled it, using the stick like a truncheon. Then I twisted it, trying to rip the arm off, but even then the creature still fought back. Finally, a major vein must have been hit. Blood shot out and the arm pulled away with the rustle of a lizard.

I could hear the mutilated monster groaning. His companions joined the lament. The pounding on the window died down. Silence. The worst sort of silence I had ever heard. I knew, I was sure, that they were out there. Suddenly, they started to whimper in unison. They meowed just like kittens calling for their mother. The meow, meow, meows were short and sweet, sad and abandoned. It was as though they were saying, Come out, come out, it's all been a misunderstanding; we didn't mean any harm. They weren't trying to be convincing, they just wanted to calm my fears. Their lethargic mews were accompanied by an occasional punch on the door or on the barred windows. Don't listen to them, for the love of God, don't listen to them, I told myself. I barricaded the door with sea chests. I put more logs on the fire in case they thought of coming down the chimney. Looking up at the ceiling made me uneasy. It was covered with slate shingles. With a bit of effort, they could break through and get in. But they didn't. During the small hours, light filtered through the cracks in the shutters with each monotonous swing of the light-house beam. Long, thin rays came and went like clockwork. They kept up the attack all through the night, first a window, then a door, and with each assault I was convinced that my barricades would give way. Afterwards, a deep quiet.

The lighthouse lantern had been extinguished. I opened a window, taking every precaution. They weren't there. A delicate margin of violet and pumpkin tones extended across the horizon. I let myself fall to the ground like a sack of potatoes, still clutching the stick. Two or three new and unfamiliar sensations battled inside me. After a while, the meagre sun rose over the water. A candle in the dark would have given off more heat than that star shrouded by a veil of clouds. But it was the sun. The summer nights were extraordinarily brief at those southern latitudes. It had been, without a doubt, the shortest night of my life. It had felt like the longest to me.

# 4

I had mastered a technique during my rebellious youth: the best way to fight sentimentalism and despair is, undoubtedly, to approach the problem in a clinical way. I devised the following hypothesis: you're dead. You find yourself on a cold and lonely island far from salvation. "You're dead, you're dead," I repeated out loud to myself as I waved a cigarette. "This is how things stand: you're dead. That means that if you don't make it, you won't have lost anything. But if you manage to survive you will have gained everything: life."

We should never underestimate the power of solitary thoughts. That cigarette magically transformed into the world's best tobacco. And the smoke coming out of my lungs was the symbol of someone who has resigned himself to fight another Thermopolis. Yes, I was worn out, but the fatigue soon dissipated. As long as I was still tired with my eyelids drooping like lead weights, I was alive. What had led me to that isolated spot didn't matter anymore. I had no past, no future. I was at the end of the world, in the middle of nowhere and far from everything. After smoking that cigarette, I felt infinitely distant from myself.

I had no illusions about my prospects. To begin with, I didn't know anything about the monsters. So, as the military manuals say, it was a worst-case scenario. Would they attack by day or night? All the time? In packs? With chaotic perseverance? How long, with my limited resources, could I hold out alone against a horde? Obviously, not very long. It was true that Gruner had managed to survive. The lighthouse was as solid as a fortress: the little house got more flimsy each time I looked at it. One thing was certain: I didn't need to ask what had happened to my predecessor.

As things stood, I had to plot some line of defence. If Gruner's fort was up in the sky, I would dig a trench in the ground. The plan was to surround the house with a moat filled with wooden spikes. That would keep the creatures at a safe distance. But the problem was time and energy: a lone man would need the strength of a mule to hollow out that much terrain. On the other hand, I had seen the monsters' pantherlike movements firsthand – the trench would have to be deep and wide. And I was exhausted, not having had an hour's sleep since my arrival. To make matters worse, I wouldn't get any rest if I was constantly working and defending myself. There were two options: be killed by the monsters, or die mad from the physical and psychological strain. It didn't take a genius to see that the two fates converged. I decided to simplify the task as much as possible. For the time being, I would concentrate on digging big holes beneath the doors and windows. I hoped it would be enough. I excavated some semicircles and filled them with sticks. After carving the wood into points with a knife, I drove the stakes down deep, spikes facing the sky. Most of the sticks were dragged off the beach. While I was by the water collecting wood, it occurred to me that the monsters' shape and webbed hands gave every indication that they came from the sea. In that case, I said to myself, fire would be a primitive but very effective weapon. It would put the theory of opposing elements into practice. And since everybody knows that all beasts have an innate fear of fire, I could only imagine the scale of its effect on amphibious creatures.

I built up my defences with stacks of wood, throwing all the books on top. A paper fire isn't as steady but it burns more intensely. Maybe that would give them a nasty jolt. Farewell, Chateaubriand! Farewell, Goethe! Farewell, Aristotle, Rilke and Stevenson. Farewell, Marx, Laforgue and Saint-Simon! Farewell, Milton, Voltaire, Rousseau, Góngora and Cervantes. How I revere you, dear friends, but art can't go before necessity; you're words. I smiled for the first time since the whole nightmare began as I stacked the piles, doused them with petrol and made bundles to add on to the future bonfire. I smiled because I had discovered while doing all this that one life, specifically my own, was worth more than the complete works of all the great thinkers, philosophers and writers of humankind.

Finally, the door. Trenching and staking out the entrance presented the clear disadvantage of blocking my own exit. So, before doing anything else, I constructed a wooden plank to bridge the gap. But I couldn't go any further, I was at my limit. I had hollowed out the earth below the windows, collected sticks, made them into lances and driven them into the ground. I had made mounds of wood and books, melding them with a stream of oil. The sun was going down. You could find fault with my reasoning, but not my instinct. Night was coming, and some gut instinct told me that darkness is ruled by butchers. Wake up, wake up, I said out loud to myself, don't fall asleep. There wasn't much water, so I splashed my face with gin. Afterwards, a void. Nothing was happening; I treated the blisters I had got on my hands from the burning log and the scratches on my neck, a souvenir of those killer claws. The pit beneath the door wasn't finished. It was the least of my worries. I had a solid barricade thanks to the heavy chests in my baggage.

I said before that the letter almost got me killed. It's one way of looking at it. That letter was the reason I had left two crates untouched. I opened them in that moment, mostly because I was afraid of falling apart if I relaxed. And I'm convinced that no one has ever, anywhere, felt such happiness as when I opened that rectangle of wood. I lifted off the cover, ripped the cardboard and found two Remington rifles wrapped in straw. The second crate contained two thousand bullets. I got down on my knees and cried like a child. It goes without saying that it was a gift from the captain. We had shared our ideas about the world on the voyage out and he knew how much I hated soldiers and anything military.

"They are a necessary evil," he would tell me.

"The worst thing about the military is that they are infantile," I answered. "The supposed honour of war boils down to being able to tell everyone about it."

We had lots of late night conversations and he knew that if he offered me a gun I would refuse it. So the captain discreetly added those crates to my luggage at the last minute. With fifty men like the captain I could found a new country, a free nation, and call it Hope.

Darkness fell. The lighthouse beam was lit. I cursed Gruner, Gruner. That name would be forever linked to dishonour. I didn't care if he was crazy, all that mattered was that he had known about the monsters and didn't tell me. I hated him with the fervour of the powerless. There was still enough time to cut a few small loopholes in the shutters; rounded incisions big enough for the barrel of a gun to stick through. And above them, some long thin slits for peepholes. But nothing happened. No movement, nor any suspicious sounds. From the window that faced the ocean you could see the coast. The water was calm and the waves, instead of pounding the sand, caressed it. I was seized by a strange feeling of impatience. If they were going to come, then let them come now. I yearned to see hundreds of monsters attacking that house. I wanted to gun them down, kill them one by one. Anything but that exasperating wait. Every one of my coat pockets was stuffed with fistfuls of bullets. The added weight felt comforting and invigorated me. Copper-coloured bullets on the left, bullets on the right, bullets in my chest pockets. I even gnawed on bullets. I clutched the rifle so tightly that the veins in my hands stood out like blue rivers. A knife and a hatchet hung off the belt strapped over my jacket. Eventually, they came.

The heads emerged first, heading toward the coast. They were like little moving buoys or advancing shark fins. There must have been ten, twenty, I don't know, schools of them. As soon as they hit the sand, the creatures turned into reptiles. Their wet skin resembled burnished steel that had been coated with oil. They dragged themselves about ten feet before standing up as perfect bipeds. But they walked slightly hunched over, like someone battling against a harsh wind. I thought of the sound of rain from the night before. Those duck feet couldn't but feel out of their element. They crushed the sand and beach stones as though treading on freshly fallen snow. A low conspiratorial hum came from their throats. That was enough for me. I opened the shutter, flinging a burning log that ignited the oil, wood, and mountains of books. I closed the shutter. My shots flew wildly from the loophole. The creatures leaped away, shrieking ferociously, like a plague of locusts. I couldn't make anything out. Just the flames that, at first, roared high. Behind the blaze were the silhouettes of bodies that jumped or danced with the fever of a witch's mass. My cries joined theirs. They bounded and squatted, came together and split apart, recoiling as they tried to reach the windows. Monsters, monsters and more monsters. Here, over there, there and here. I went from one window to another. I fired blind, one, two, three, and four shots, swearing like a Berber against Rome as I reloaded. Shooting and reloading for hours on end, or maybe it was just a few minutes, I don't know.

The bonfires began to die down. I saw that the fire protected my morale more than anything else. But they had vanished. I didn't realise it at first. I kept on shooting until the rifle jammed. I fumbled the catch frenetically. It wouldn't release – where was the other Remington? The cylindrical cartridges scattered under my feet made me slip and stumble. The bullets rolled around in my pockets. I wanted to pick them up, but the good bullets and the spent cartridges were all jumbled together. I dragged myself over to the ammunition box, put my hand in and grabbed a handful of icy lead, taking my time. I sensed, to my surprise, that the monsters had stopped wailing. Panting like a beaten dog, I peered out of the loopholes. There was no enemy to be seen from my angle of vision. The flames had faded from red to blue and barely flickered a foot high. They crackled. The lighthouse beam swept the landscape with an even cadence. What horrors were they devising? Nothing was to be trusted. Darkness continued to erode the landscape.

A distant explosion pierced through the layers of mist. What was it? Gruner and his rifle. They were attacking the lighthouse. I stopped and listened. The frenzied sounds of combat were carried over by gusts of wind. On the other side of the island, the monsters roared with the force of a hurricane. Gruner spaced out his gunshots as if he were only aiming at sure targets. The inhuman screams rose in volume with each blast. But the way Gruner wielded his rifle revealed a quiet assurance. He acted more with the ease of a lion tamer than someone teetering on the brink. I'd almost say that I heard him laugh, but I wouldn't swear to it.


Dawn: light filtered through floury gauze. The blisters on my hands had swollen up, despite all the bandages and ointments. I supposed it was from gripping the gun so tightly all night. My breath stank like stale tobacco. Bile that tasted like burnt sugar welled up in my mouth. My overall condition was deplorable. Weakness in the knees. Loosely strung muscles. Blurry vision with yellow sparks. The piles of logs and books were still smoking. I set to work excavating a pit at the foot of the door. However, at midmorning I was interrupted by a completely unexpected visit.

Gruner was the perfect image of a Siberian hunter, fat and surly. He wore a felt cap with big earflaps and a coat sewn up with thick thread; lots of buckles. His chest was crisscrossed with lacing. He was carrying a rifle and a sort of harpoon strapped on his back. The lighthouse keeper moved slowly but assuredly, swaying like an elephant bowed down by his weight. My body was half in, half out of the pit. I stopped shovelling.

"Nice fellows, aren't they? Those toads I mean," he said in an almost friendly way, and then added, coldly, "I thought you would be dead by now. Here," he said, passing me a bucket with a sack of beans inside, "you can use the fountain too."

His words were in the same tone that is used with the dying: give them anything but the truth.

"I need something more than beans and a water fountain, Gruner," I said while still in the ditch. "The lighthouse, Gruner, the lighthouse. Without the lighthouse I'm a dead man."

"It's going to rain tonight," he commented, looking up at the sky. "That drives them away."

"Be reasonable," I protested with trembling lips. "What's the sense of struggling alone? Humans need to unite when they're surrounded by predators."

"Take all the water you want; it's yours, honestly. And the beans. I also have coffee. Want coffee? You'll need coffee."

"Why are you pushing me away? You should judge me by my intentions, not my presence."

"Your very presence shows your intentions. You can't understand. You'd never be able to understand."

"The problem," I said, "is whether we can come to an understanding."

"The problem," he said, "is that I'm stronger."

It was unbelievable. I screamed, "Allowing a man to die is the same as killing him! You're an assassin! An assassin! Any court in the world would condemn you! By action or omission you're throwing me into the lion's pit. You hole up in your lighthouse and contemplate the spectacle like a patrician at the Colosseum. Are you happy, Gruner?" I fumed with growing indignation.

He got down on his knees. Suddenly, we were face to face. He touched the fingers of both hands together and cleared his throat. My protests hadn't had any effect on him.

"No one else goes in that lighthouse. That's a fact. You have to accept it, not understand it." He paused for a long moment without daring to look at me with his small, beady eyes. Then, "I heard shots yesterday. I wonder if our weaponry is compatible . . ."

Gruner left the sentence unfinished, leaving me to fill in the rest. He had been struggling on the island for a long time and was surely beginning to run low on bullets. It was the height of depravity. Although he made it clear that my life meant nothing to him, he was asking for ammunition to defend his own. And in exchange for a bag of beans. I threw a shovelful of dirt in his face.

"Here! Is that compatible enough for you? Criminal!" I climbed out of the pit. I kicked the bucket and the beans went flying. That gesture managed to unsettle him more than any argument.

"I have no quarrel with you! No matter what you may think, I mean you no harm. I am not a murderer." He said this while taking the harpoon off his back. It was an unspoken threat, but the weapon was there between us, grasped in his two hands.

"Get out, out!" I yelled with my arm outstretched, just as one would throw a beggar out of an expensive restaurant. Gruner did not budge. He held his ground for a few seconds more, unwilling to abandon his mission.

"Be gone, you human vermin, out!" I moved toward him with determination. Gruner backed away slowly, facing me all the while. He turned and walked away with absolute indifference.

"You shall pay dearly for this one day, Gruner; you shall pay for it all!" I cursed before he disappeared into the forest. He did not deign to reply.

Now I was certain that they attacked only at night. It

was true that Gruner had come armed, but it was surely to defend himself against me, not the monsters. Otherwise, he wouldn't have been moving so freely about the island. Unfortunately, I arrived at these conclusions too late. I feared that my first slumber would be my last. Would I be able to wake myself up when night fell? What was to stop me, in my exhaustion, from falling into a deadly stupor? My own vulnerability terrified me as much as the monsters. And despite all this, I was overcome throughout the day by moments of weakness. One couldn't say that I truly slept. It was a drugged grogginess, more akin to delirium tremens than to actual slumber. A strange mix of visions, memories, mirages and meaningless hallucinations appeared before me, on the frontiers of consciousness. I couldn't be sure, but it seemed to be a stretch of the docks of Amsterdam, or perhaps it was Dublin. Pools of oil floated on the water's surface, washing up against the wooden pilings and echoing hollowly. I could see myself, as if from above, in the house on the island. A demon in human form was asleep on my bunk. I could have practically reached out and touched it with my fingertips. I woke up, more or less. I do not want to die. What shall become of me, what will they do to me?

The third night arrived without reprieve. Buckets of rain poured just as Gruner had predicted. Thunder and lightning.

Banks of clouds hung low with white blazes above them, wide as lakes and fleeting as dud fireworks. The thunder pounded like a hammer smashing a thousand-piece dinner service to bits. The churning waves were visible from the loopholes. The night-time horizon was resplendent like a battleship in the heat of combat. The lightning ripped through the sky, falling in jagged and scattered verticality.

Later, the rain lessened into a hazy, damp curtain. It was impossible to see more than a few inches beyond the windowpanes. Drops of water bounced off the slate roof. Raucous torrents sluiced down the gutters. This time I did not see them coming. Suddenly, the door became a marching drum for dozens of angry fists. The barricade of crates and chests gave way under the force of the pounding, and my body with it. I fell down on my knees. A malignant force caused me to crumple and give in. That infernal beating weakened the door even as it shook my spirits.

The horrors of the world were reunited in that shuddering portal. I was beyond hope, beyond madness; but I had yet to give up. I had not yet reached such sublime indifference and refused to go quietly to my fate. The monsters' cries ceased. All that could be heard was the deluge of fists, one punch on top of another. I whimpered a little as I chewed on a clenched fist, with the knowledge that no amount of good fortune would be enough to get me off that island. The door began to give way. It trembled like a laurel leaf in a boiling pot and would shatter any minute. Locked in a sort of paralysed entrancement, I was unable to take my eyes off that door. And a miracle occurred in those last moments, but it was the opposite of what one would expect.

I was no longer in need of salvation; it was pointless. In a few seconds, I should be carrion. The miracle was this: that I no longer cared. In fact, I was dead already. Being dead, I no longer felt it necessary to curl up in a corner. In light of the situation, it seemed ludicrous. I was dead, but I had ceased to tremble. I was dead, but before I reached oblivion, it was my lot to experience the very nature of the abyss. What else could that quaking door be other than raw horror itself? My body felt so weak that I had to crawl across the floor. My last wish was to touch that door with my fingertips. It was as though its touch would release some source of universal wisdom: an ever present knowledge accessible only to those who had been received in palaces of light. I was mere inches away. I raised my palm in front of the door as though it were glass, not wood. But in that exact moment one of the monsters smashed the slit that served as a lookout. An arm slipped through the gap, slithered down like a salamander's tail and grabbed my wrist.

"No!"

In the blink of an eye, I fell from the loftiest spirituality to the basest animal instincts. No, no, I had no wish to die. I bit down into that hand with every tooth. The small bones crunched as I ripped the membrane that joined the first two fingers. The beast cried out with a long, unending howl of pain, and yet I refused to let go. I pulled back with my jaw, pressing down with my heels until I felt something give way. My head hit the floor due to the sudden impulse. My face and chest were soaked in blue blood; it dripped off my chin and elbows. I reeled like a drunken orang-utan, incapable of putting myself to rights. Later, days later, I realised that those awful sounds had escaped from my gritted teeth. I happened to rest my hands on one of the rifles. I loaded it like a blind man, without looking, and then fired shots through the door. The bullets perforated the wood. Yellowish shavings flew everywhere. The monsters yelped in a frustrated pack. The door had been reduced to a slice of Swiss cheese. The beasts had gone, but I kept on shooting. The storm was moving off. By dawn, the rain was only a light drizzle. It was only when it grew light that I noticed how rigid my mouth was, as though it were packed full of something. I spat out half a finger and a membrane bigger than a Brazilian butterfly.

The last flash of lightning illuminated my mind. I had a thousand nameless monsters against me. But they weren't really my true enemies any more than an earthquake has a vendetta against buildings. They simply existed.

I had only one enemy and his name was Gruner, Gruner. The lighthouse, the lighthouse, the lighthouse.

# 5

I had never been a very good shot, but I was determined to learn. One catches on quickly in cases of emergency. I calibrated the Remington's scope and took aim at empty tins of spinach. Here I was met with my first obstacle. I practised all morning with limited success. My mind and body were in an equally sorry state. A crushing fatigue wore on my senses. On shutting one eye to take aim, my vision doubled. My nerves were crumbling at a rapid rate. Mortal danger was compounded by the infamous torture of insomnia. My body's natural physiological rhythms had ceased to function. I ordered my body about as a colonel commands a regiment. Eat. Drink. Walk. Urinate. Do not give in to sleep! My horror of sleep was as pressing as the need for it. I inhabited a mental realm where the borders between insomnia and sleepwalking blurred. Occasionally, I would tell myself to do this or that, to load the rifle or light a cigarette. But the bullets refused to enter the chamber; the gun was already loaded and I had no recollection of having done so. I would put a cigarette to my lips, only to realise that I was smoking one already.

But now I had embarked on a mission. Survival had been my sole concern until that moment, with no glimpse of hope on the horizon. For the first time, I was driven by some sense of purpose. My mind made up, I charged as fearlessly as a warrior through the forest. As much as my wardrobe allowed, I had chosen clothing in tones that would blend in with the surrounding vegetation. Leather gloves would help withstand the cold and blisters. I took up a position sixty yards from the lighthouse. The site would have been coveted by any marksman. A dense thicket at my back kept the light from filtering through and casting my shadow. I secreted myself behind the last line of foliage, always keeping watch on the door and balcony. Then I clambered up into a tree. The thickly gnarled branch had a hollow which made an ideal cradle for the rifle. I took aim at the door. Gruner would be a dead man if he so much as showed himself. But there was no sign of life in the lighthouse all day. Gruner did not make an appearance. For fear of the monsters, I had no choice but to abandon my watch as dusk fell.

Fortunately, it was a quiet night, if one may call it such. The beasts did not attack my cottage. I assumed some had circled the lighthouse, given the ruckus and a distant shot from Gruner, but that was all. It seemed impossible to draw any conclusions. Perhaps they had had enough. The shots fired through the door were certain to have wounded some of them. The fact that Gruner was saving his bullets may have drawn them to the lighthouse. Perhaps it was simply that they hadn't worked up much of an appetite that evening. Who knew? It went against all logic, let alone military strategy. I even allowed myself the luxury of closing my eyes before dawn, a false but ever so seductive repose. At the first glimmer of daylight, I repositioned myself back in my tree.

This time, I did not have long to wait. Scarcely half an hour had passed when Gruner appeared on the balcony. Half naked, he bared the torso of a retired boxer to the world and leaned against the rusty railing, his arms spread wide apart. Gruner stood stock-still with his chin up and eyes shut, drinking in our meagre sun's rays. The man resembled a figure from Madame Tussaud's. His skin was perfectly white. He made an ideal target. I set the rifle against my shoulder and snapped my right eye shut. The muzzle trained directly on his chest. But I hesitated. What if I missed? What if I merely injured him? It made no difference if the wound was grave or superficial. All would be lost if Gruner managed to find refuge inside. No matter how long the agony, he would have already barricaded the balcony. Yes, the walls could be scaled with some rope and a hook. But one could never force open the sheets of steel shuttering the balcony's windows. As I told myself all this I also said: No, that is not the real reason and you know it.

I was simply incapable of killing the man. As much as

circumstances impelled me, I was not an assassin. Shooting a man was a great deal more than taking aim; it was the act of killing every remaining hour of his life. While Gruner lay in my viewfinder, I could envisage his entire biography. I imagined his existence prior to the lighthouse. Against my will, my mind recreated Gruner's stupefaction as a child; the journey which, in the still distant future, would lead him to the island. Every failure of his youth and all the disappointments and frustrations inflicted by a world he had never chosen. How many beatings had he received from those very same hands meant to nurture him? Now that he was reduced to a defenceless target, his vulnerability was patently clear. What had brought Gruner to the lighthouse? Was he in himself cruel or did he carry cruelty like a disease, spreading it to others? Gruner was simply a man basking half naked in the sun. He wore no uniform that would justify the bullet. And no matter how one looked at it, to rob a human life was in itself a painful task. However, to kill a man who was merely sunbathing was nothing less than abominable.

I climbed down from the tree, deeply ashamed of myself. On the way back to the house, I chastised myself by pounding my head with my fists. Fool, I cursed at myself, you are a fool. The monsters don't distinguish between saints and sinners. It is all the same meat to them. You are on the island, the island of infamy. No good man, no philosopher, poet or philanthropist could survive in this place, only

Gruner. I took the path that led to the house and stopped in my tracks at the spring. I brought Gruner's bucket, still lying on the ground, to my lips. But I caught my reflection in the water before taking a sip.

My visage was scarcely recognisable. Days of insomnia and combat had wreaked their havoc. I had a scraggly beard and my face was pale, deathly pale. My eyes especially were haunted by a look of irretrievable lunacy. My blue irises were islands hemmed in by deep crimson. A series of dark violet rings jockeyed for position in and around my eye sockets. My lips were cracked by a combination of cold and fear. The scarflike bandage on my neck oozed pus and clots of barely dried blood. My body had lost the art of healing itself. I had broken nails and my hair was coated in what appeared to be a tarlike substance. I snatched a clump from behind my ear and saw, with great puzzlement, that its shade had turned a snowy grey. I dunked my head into the bucket and scrubbed frantically. It did little good. My anatomy lay buried in filth of biblical proportions. I laid the rifle, ammunition and knives down and stripped off my clothing as if each garment were ridden with plague. Then I scaled the rock face where the water sprang forth.

A kind of pool had been formed by the night before last's rain on that upper plateau. The water barely grazed my knees. I dropped down in to it. The frigid water had a benign influence. I was glad of it, for the cold would sharpen and invigorate my senses. Naturally, my thoughts were fixed on Gruner. The spring might serve as an excellent trap. He was bound to come by for water before long. An ambush. Gruner would be defenceless and caught unawares. He could be captured at gunpoint and there would be no need for murder. I would force him to surrender; take him prisoner. Chains stored in the lighthouse would become his fetters. And at the first sighting of a ship, I would use the lighthouse's beam to flash a message in Morse code. Should Gruner be tried in a court of law or locked up for life in an insane asylum? That was secondary.

Fine yet tangible columns of light filtered through the clouds. Soft lichen, pleasing to the touch, covered the edges of the pool. I was in no hurry to leave the water. My limbs had grown accustomed to its temperature. I floated on the surface, gazing at the firmament above: it was my first moment of pleasure since disembarking.

I was still bobbing about when I heard some footsteps coming closer. I submerged myself up to the neck to avoid detection. The sound of clanking tin revealed that Gruner carried more buckets. What was to be done? It was just a matter of time before he discovered my clothing and, what was worse, my rifle. It was uncertain what his reaction would be. We might yet be able to share the spring without conflict. But lunatics are a sensitive lot. He certainly considered himself capable of surmising my intentions. And I went unarmed. There was no time to reflect on the situation. The fact was that my options were limited. Even if by some miracle Gruner left without noticing the clothing, he would not return for days. Meanwhile, the monsters would have infinite opportunities to annihilate me. I strained to listen. He was just in front of the pipe; I could hear him change one pail for another. A sudden quiet fell. The fellow was sure to have seen my clothing by now. I bounded in one pantherlike leap, and our two bodies were rolling together on the ground. I managed to get the upper hand and seized my combatant's legs. My raised fist froze in midair. This was not Gruner. It was a monster.

I leapt back as far as I could. But I did so in confusion. Monsters were killing machines. The body I had wrestled with was lightweight and fragile. The buckets continued to roll about on the ground, banging against each other with the din of a pedlar's cart. I kept a prudent distance while observing the monster, like a cat frozen by curiosity.

The beast lay where it had fallen, letting out the pitiful sounds of a wounded bird. The stench of fish invaded my nostrils. I dragged myself over to the beast and pried its hands from its face in order to observe it more closely. There was no doubt that it was one of the monsters. But its facial features softened the overall effect prodigiously. Its rounded face ended in a bald skull. The eyebrows were lines that appeared to have been drawn by some Sumerian calligrapher.

Its eyes were blue; by God, were they blue. The very blue of an African sky. No; it was brighter, purer, more intense and brilliant. The subtle nose was thin and pointed with high-set nostrils. The ears were smaller than any human's and were shaped like fishtails, each one being divided into four tiny vertebrae. It had smooth cheeks and a long, thin neck. The monster's entire body was covered in a creamy grey skin tinged with touches of green. Ever wary, I touched the flesh with my fingertips. It was as cold as a corpse and had a snaky texture. I examined one of its hands. It differed greatly from the other monsters. The webbing barely reached its finger knuckles. A panicked scream escaped from its lips. Inexplicably, that touch drove me to beat the thing mercilessly, I know not why. It cried and whimpered, covered only in an old sweater, shapeless enough to serve as a dress. I picked it up by its ankle, holding the thing like an infant so as to observe it more closely. Yes, it was female. The genitals were bare, untrammeled by pubic hair. Its legs kicked desperately. I punished the little beast with the rifle barrel until a particularly cruel blow to the groin caused it to curl up like a worm. Face to the ground, the beast whimpered and covered its head in its hands.

The jersey and the bucket indicated that Gruner was in some way connected to the little beast. Where had she been found and what value did he place on her? It was impossible to tell. The fact was that she had been trained, much like a Saint Bernard, to complete a few basic tasks. She collected the water, for example. He had also taken the trouble to dress her, although the outfit was one even a beggar would scorn. The combination of such a dirty and torn jersey and her amphibious form was insufferable; far worse than those little dogs that the English dress up in the best tweeds. But if Gruner had bothered at all, then the monster surely meant something to him. The best way to find out was to take her hostage. If he had any interest, Gruner would come looking for her. She trembled as I put a bucket over her head as a blinder. The buckets were linked with a rope which served to bind her hands behind her back. I purposely left signs of struggle. Gruner would see what had happened and come looking for us. One smack of the rifle barrel and we were on our way toward the cottage.

I sat her down on a stool. After removing the bucket from her head I took a seat and observed her for quite some time. The corners of her lips were crusted with blue blood. Her heart pounded as swiftly as a rabbit's, and her breathing was shallow. I was met with an empty gaze. Her eyes followed vaguely as I waved a finger in front of her like a hypnotist. Then the thing wet herself on the stool. I kept watch out the window facing the forest path.

Gruner did not come. My irritation mounted. One horribly violent blow from my fist sent her flailing on the ground. This time, the monster did not make a sound. She remained huddled in a corner, attempting to protect herself with manacled hands.

It was past midday. The light was fading with still no sign of Gruner. Naturally, I had no intention of keeping the female. The monsters were to be feared even under normal conditions. What would they be capable of if they realised that I held one of their own kind captive? Her skin was like a dolphin's; taut like the strings of a violin. She appeared to be a young and fertile creature. Nature is endlessly inventive as to its techniques of reproduction. Perhaps she could communicate with her companions through some chemical mechanism undetectable to humans. I was on the verge of putting the beast out of her misery.

The sound of gunfire pierced through the window just as the sun had begun to set.

"Rat bastard!" bellowed an unseen voice. "Why declare war on me? Are not the toads enough?"

"And what about you, Gruner?" I called out into the void. "You would rather waste what little ammunition you have left on me?"

"Thief! *Sie bescheissenes Arschloch!*"

Another shot rang out. The bullet lodged itself in the upper corner of the window frame, bringing down a rain of wood shavings. I pressed the little beast against the window.

"Fire away, Gruner! With luck you may hit your target!"

"Let her go!"

I wrenched her arm by way of an answer. The beast shrieked. Indignant cries could be heard from somewhere in the undergrowth. That was precisely the response I had sought. My laughter rang out.

"What seems to be the trouble, Gruner? You don't like my antics? Well then, listen to this!" My boot trod down hard on her naked foot, sending yelps of pain through the woods.

"Stop! Do not kill her! What do you want? Tell me what you want!"

"I want to talk. Face to face!"

"Show yourself and we will talk!"

He had not formulated his all-too-quick reply and its insincerity was patently obvious.

"The only one who will show himself is you. Now!"

He did not reply. My greatest concern was that Gruner might simply walk away. He had no reason to persist. It was inconceivable. Many a farmer may be capable of murdering a neighbour over a cow. But not one of them would risk his life for a wolf. In my possession was a thing whose value I could not gauge.

I seemed to hear some branches move outside.

"Gruner, come out immediately."

I pulled his pet away from the window in order to speak. I saw the double barrel of his shotgun emerging from the bushes, lit up by flashes of sulphur. Gruner's bullets were authentic fragmentary shells. He missed me by a hair. The cornice of the window frame shattered; a sliver of wood lodged itself in one of my eyebrows. The wound, though insignificant in itself, enraged me. I threw the beast to the ground like a rag, pressing her down with the heel of my boot. My hands were then left free to wield the rifle. The surrounding greenery was cascaded with lead. I held the firearm up to my chest, covering every possible angle. Gruner could be anywhere, but at the very least he would be forced to take cover. I called out and was met with no response. What was he playing at? Assault or siege? Had he the will to conduct a prolonged attack? I had no choice but to leap from one window to another, with baited breath. If Gruner managed to reach that outer wall, my position would no longer be safe. I spotted him behind me. He was skulking around the house by way of the beach so as to catch me unawares. I fired, but he was shielded by an embankment.

"I shall murder you," he swore, huddled over. "By God, I shall destroy you!"

The fellow's position belied his words: Gruner was trapped. It would be difficult to take aim while he stayed on the sand. But he would be forced to leave the beach sooner or later. When that time came, he would be a sitting duck, regardless of where he went. It was far worse to remain where he was. Come nightfall, the monsters would surely be delighted to find his prone body on the shore.

"You must give up!" I told him. "Surrender or I shall kill you both!"

With unexpected determination and speed, Gruner risked an escape. He ran doubled over, screaming in an oddly high, girlish voice. I could fire only two shots. The bullets went astray in the ocean as he disappeared into foliage.

The crossfire ended there. Had he gone back to the lighthouse? Perhaps that is what he would like me to think. I tied a cord around the hostage's neck and secured her to a bed leg. Then I shoved open the door and pushed her outside. Gruner was sure to be disturbed by the sight and might do something foolhardy. Thinking she was free, the beast hesitated before running a few yards. The rope pulled tight with a jolt, throwing the little thing to the ground.

All was still for several minutes. I kept an eye out of the window, observing the beast lying bound and listless on the ground. She strained on the rope off and on, like a chained dog in search of its owner. Then she would give up, rest and make another attempt. All at once, the rope was severed by a well-placed bullet. An excellent shot! What happened next can only be justified by mutual madness. We both made a mad dash for the hostage instead of firing at each other. Each of us abandoned our respective hideouts of house and forest, but Gruner was farther away. I grasped the beast's neck in one hand and the rifle in the other. She did not resist. My arm had not the strength to fire the weapon as a pistol and I missed. Gruner's entire body was in movement, a ball of fur and hair tossed by the wind with the ever present harpoon on his shoulder. He could not shoot me for fear of injuring the very being he was trying to save.

"Give up!" I warned. "It is no use!"

He spat at me before zigzagging rapidly into the forest. I learned the truth of a very old lesson: it is no simple thing to kill a man who knows how to move. I returned to my refuge, using the rifle barrel to prod the hostage inside.

Evening fell over the earth like a net of darkness. I watched the forest furtively, gripping my rifle on an island infested by monsters, a specimen of wild sea vermin at my side. It was all too fantastic to be believed. Not four days ago I had been discussing politics with a sea captain. First I would tell myself that none of it was real. Then I would say, yes, yes it was. I argued with the world as to its plausibility until a sharp blast jolted me out of such musings. Dusk had settled in.

I was just beginning to worry more about the monsters than about Gruner when a booming voice cried, "How do I know you will not shoot?"

"Because I've had the opportunity to annihilate you many times over, and yet you are still alive!" I answered swiftly. "You fancy a nice sunbath, Gruner? Do you enjoy going out on your balcony in the morning half naked? Many a time I have had you in my sights. I just had to press the trigger." Then, barking like a sergeant, I said, "Show yourself for once, damn you. Come out!"

At long last, he left the woods, but not without some reluctance.

"Throw the rifle aside," I ordered, "and get on your knees."

He obeyed grudgingly. Kneeling but unshaken, Gruner spread his arms wide as if to say: Here I am.

"Now it's your turn to show yourself," he demanded with his hands on the back of his neck, "and bring her with you!"

I put the beast in front of me like a shield. When we grew near, I shoved her toward Gruner, aiming the rifle at them both. Gruner inspected the beast as a veterinarian might examine a sickly goat.

"Look what you have done, she's covered in bruises!" he protested.

"What did you expect? The monsters have blue blood, after all," I said with cruel irony. Gruner's gaze ranged widely until his eyes finally rested on me.

"Very well, it's getting dark. What is it you want?"

"You should know by now."

I sat down with the rifle across my lap. Suddenly, if

one may say so, the situation became almost restful. Not a moment before, we had been about to cut each other's throats, and suddenly we were practically chatting. We resembled a pair of Phoenicians who had worn themselves out in a theatrical and not very heartfelt bout of haggling. The island was an uncanny place.

"I should kill you right now, but I won't," I began in a conciliatory tone. "To be honest, I care not a whit as to what is happening on this devilish island. For reasons unknown to me, you do not wish to abandon it. You had the opportunity when I disembarked and said nothing. Very well, remain if you wish. I, on the other hand, intend to escape from this place safe and sound."

I pointed in the direction of the lighthouse. "I mean to get in there, with or without you. Get in and survive. A ship is bound to pass by soon. We shall use the lighthouse's beam to send an SOS and I will depart to some more tranquil place. That is all. Naturally, you may keep my provisions and the weapons. I have two Remington rifles and thousands of bullets. I am sure you will find them useful."

I caught a glimpse of rotten teeth as his mouth twisted into an enigmatic smile. He took a swig from a small iron flask without offering me any. "You don't understand. This island lies far beyond any commercial route. The only ship that will enter these waters will be the one bringing the replacement weather official. A year from now."

"You cannot fool me! There is a lighthouse here. And lighthouses are strategically placed on shipping routes."

He shook his head, threw aside the cigarette he had been smoking and said, "I assure you, the route has been in disuse for ages. They had originally planned on building a jail here for prisoners of the Boer War. Something along those lines anyway, I don't know. But the nautical charts were out of date and miscalculated the island's size. This rock doesn't even have room for a guardhouse. They believed it to be much larger" – sweeping his hand in an all-inclusive motion – "and the building contract was handed over to a private company. The surveyors realised as soon as they arrived that the project wasn't feasible and rushed to get the budget approved before some general cancelled the whole endeavour. The lighthouse was included in the plans for the prison. They decided to build so as not to be accused of siphoning funds from the military budget. I imagine it all worked out on paper. They built the lighthouse and went away."

He sighed sarcastically. "They might have spared themselves the trouble. No public works inspector would ever have come here. Especially once the English ceded control of the lighthouse over to international domain. What does that actually mean anyway? What once belonged to an army is now the property of no one."

He sat back down. Indeed, none of it made sense.

"I refuse to believe it! If that is how things stand, then what are you doing here? You are the keeper of a lighthouse without ships?"

His moods were changeable. Gruner had feared the worst concerning the little beast, and getting her back had soothed his spirits. He laughed and this time passed me the flask. The liquor was bitter and cold, but I valued his gesture much more than any drink.

"I was not sent to man the lighthouse. I am the former weather official. Well, to be honest I am not actually qualified for the post, but the company was not exactly picky about the sort of personnel they sent here." He paused. "One of the sailors on the boat that brought me over, some South African who knew the tale, told me all about the lighthouse."

He motioned for the flask and took a swig.

"And you, friend? Why have you come here? Victors are not wont to disembark in these climes. Ever. Nor honest or upright men. And you? Did your wife leave you for some railroad engineer? Or perhaps you lost a fortune in the casino. On second thought, don't tell me. It is all the same. Welcome to the hell of outcasts, the paradise of the damned," – and, shifting abruptly his tone and manner – "Where is the other Remington?"

Overcome by fatigue, I let him have his way. Gruner's little beast stared at the ground with a bovine indifference, sliding her fingers around in the mud. She swallowed an insect whole. Gruner went inside the house. He kneeled before the crate of bullets just like a pirate marvelling over a treasure chest. The sight of rifle and ammunition filled him with glee. "This is good, very good," he said as one hand stroked the rifle, while his other fingered the bullets like a miser with his gold.

"Lend me a hand!" he said abruptly. "It will be dark soon. You realise what that means, don't you?"

Gruner slung his own rifle and the other Remington over his shoulders. Together, we carried the ammunition box by its side handles. Yes, it was growing dark. He shoved the mascot ahead and the three of us began a mad dash. "Make haste, hurry," Gruner spurred me on as we rushed through the forest. "The lighthouse, the lighthouse." He muttered the same words in German: "*Zum Leuchtturm, zum Leuchtturm!*" It was an awkward business to coordinate our four legs and I tripped over a root. The ammunition scattered. "What the devil is the matter with you?" he swore while snatching up fistfuls of bullets. "Are you drunk?" The box contained a muddied jumble of moss and bullets. We began to run. Night was upon us. "Oh Lord, oh dear Lord," Gruner whispered. *"Zum Leuchtturm, zum Leuchtturm!"*

We were but twenty yards away from the lighthouse and had just begun the sharp ascent up its foundation of natural rock when Gruner screamed, "Shoot, shoot!" I did

not know what he meant. "Behind the lighthouse, you fool!"
I could distinguish about four or five vague shadows flicking
around on all sides. My rifle let loose a wild volley of bullets.
The monsters knew well the firearm's power and fled as a
pack. Gruner had taken charge of the crate. "Open the door,
it is unlocked!" he cried.

Not a second after we barred the door, the monsters
began to pound the sheets of iron with apocalyptic fury.
Gruner hovered over the ammunition, but I interposed
myself between him and the bullets.

"What now?" he protested. "They are attacking the
lighthouse; I need the bullets!"

"Look me in the eye."

"Why?"

"Look me in the eye."

"What do you want from me?"

"That you look me in the eye."

He did it. I set the muzzle of his rifle against my chest.

"You wish to see me dead? Then do it. I can't abide
the thought of being murdered in my bed. If you mean to
kill me, do it now. It shall make you an assassin, but at least
you shan't be a traitor."

Gruner panted furiously, unsure of how to respond to
such a vague insult. He ripped the weapon out of my hands
and in one rough movement pressed it into my temple. The
metal was cold. "You are the sort who wants to live forever.

Did your dear parents never read you the words of Christ? They never taught you that our fate is to die many times over?" He pulled the weapon away and lowered his eyes. "Every one of us must die. Providence decrees whether it is today or tomorrow. We each have a rifle. Kill me if that is what you wish."

Gruner's rough-hewn features dissolved into an unexpected smile. He paused in silence, ignoring the urgency of our situation. The shrieking continued outside as Gruner subjected me to a hermetic scrutiny. At last he said, "You sought refuge in the lighthouse and here you are. Do you expect my congratulations? You don't understand a thing. You are the sort of man who has to get right up against the bars of a prison in order to feel free." He gestured greedily. "And now, let me at the bullets. The toads are on their way."

I stepped aside and gave him what he wanted. Gruner bounded lightly up the stairs, despite the heavy burden of his rifle, the Remington and the ammunition box. I noticed a pair of empty sacks and put them to use as an improvised mattress. The monsters howled. I heard shots being fired from somewhere on high. But I could think only of sleep.

Sleep.

Sleep.

Sleep.

# 6

An uncanny tranquillity reigned over the earth when I awoke. At some point in the night, my body had been resurrected like Lazarus. Outside, the waves crashed gently against the rocks nearby. The seaside sounds had a calming effect. From my supine position, the lighthouse's interior gave the impression of being at once sturdy and welcoming. Shafts of light fell from various heights through the windows, which followed the twists of the spiral staircase. I watched motes of dust drift slowly in a nearby beam. They floated with an absurd and melancholy harmony. My mouth was dry. I sat up and drank from a nearby jug. It was vinegar, but it made no difference. I would have drunk it even if it were boiling oil. My every movement set off a series of shooting pains. Thousands of needles tingled in each limb, as though my blood hadn't circulated in years. I took note of my changed surroundings while still sitting on those sacks. There was hardly any space left at the base of the lighthouse. It was packed full with crates, sacks and trunks. I looked closer. They were mine. Just then, Gruner came through the door.

"How the devil did you lug all of that in half a morning's time?" I asked in a groggy voice.

"You have been asleep for fifty hours," Gruner answered as he dropped a sack of flour.

I looked down at my hands and said dully, "I am famished."

"I am sure you are."

Gruner gave me no further sign; nevertheless, I followed him up the stairs.

Without stopping or turning around, he said, "You didn't hear them? Not even a bit? It was quite a near thing last night. Lately they have been more vicious than ever." And, under his breath, "The worst of the worst."

He lifted the trapdoor and we entered the living quarters. He pointed to the table and chair and ordered me to sit down. I obeyed. Gruner remained standing, gazing out over the balcony and packing his pipe. I rubbed my face and leaned my elbows on the table. A dish was placed in front of me by a set of thin webbed fingers. Those hands were not human. My first reaction was to jump out of the chair with a screech of fear. My heart thundered against my chest. That was life on the island.

"There is no need to yell," said Gruner. "It is only pea soup."

Gruner smacked his lips like a peasant calling to his mule. The little beast vanished down the trapdoor. We said no more until I had finished eating.

"Thank you for the soup."

"That soup was yours."

"Well, thank you for offering it to me."

"She is the one that served you."

The beast was neither chained nor bound. I asked, "Doesn't she ever try to escape from the lighthouse?"

"Does a dog ever run away from its master?"

There was a space of silence and I couldn't help betraying a certain animosity. "And what other abilities does she have, apart from carrying dishes and pails? Have you also taught her Latin?"

Gruner gave me a hard stare. He didn't want a row, but he wasn't afraid of answering back. "No, neither Greek nor Latin. This is the only thing I have taught her" – lifting the Remington up – "and it is worth all of the classics put together."

"Of course," I said, rubbing my forehead. A horrible migraine impeded me from following his words closely.

"But if I must answer your question, I will say yes. She does have some abilities that make her invaluable. She sings whenever the toads are nearby."

"Sings?"

"Sings. Like a canary." He could not suppress a deep, macabre and very ugly shadow of a laugh. "I fancy that she brings her owner good luck. She is the best mascot to be found in these parts."

Nothing more was said. I sat quietly in my chair. I wasn't thinking clearly. It was difficult for me to associate images with their corresponding words. I was as shocked and disconcerted as the survivor of an avalanche. My gaze wandered around the room: from the bed, the balcony, to Gruner's immobile figure, and none of it had any real meaning.

"Perhaps we should take stock," Gruner said, mistaking my stupefaction for passivity. "Follow me."

We ascended the iron staircase that led up to the top floor. The beacon's lenses were housed there, in the cupola of the lighthouse. It was a complex clockwork mechanism made from massive pieces of industrial steel. Metal axles connected the lenses to a generator in the centre of the room. The moving parts were set on a sort of miniature railway which circled the perimeter of the room. Gruner adjusted three levers and the whole thing began to move, sputtering to life with a chorus of elephantine creaking and grating.

"As you can see, I have calibrated the angle of the lenses so as to track the lighthouse's immediate surroundings. That way, one may spot the toads before they get too close. The angle of the lenses changes with each revolution and their beam moves back and forth from the lighthouse's base to points farther off. One may sweep the entire forest. The beam can even reach the weather official's house on the other extreme of the island if necessary."

"I am fully aware of that."

Even I wasn't sure to what extent my words were a recrimination or simply a statement of fact. Gruner did not capture either meaning.

"The beacon could be set to train steadily on the door below. But what would be the use? They would only dodge the beams. As it is, every swing of the lamp gets them scampering about. They abhor light, human or divine, as all infernal beasts do."

The tower was the highest elevation on the island, affording a magnificent view of our surroundings. The land spread out in the shape of a sock. The slate shingles of the weather official's cottage stood out against the turn in the sock's heel. All along the coast, on both sides of the island, reefs of ranging shapes and sizes speckled the ocean. One promontory extended beyond the others on the northern shore, about 100 or 150 yards into the water. On closer inspection, I saw the wrecked prow of a small ship.

"It was a Portuguese ship," Gruner informed me before I had the chance to ask. "The wreck happened not long ago. The vessel embarked from their colony in Mozambique and was heading for southern Chile. The ship was carrying contraband. That is why it took this desolate route. The small vessel ran into trouble, and was trying to reach Bouvet Island. But it ran against the rocks." He concluded the tale with the same indifference as if he were recalling some minor incident from childhood.

"I suppose that, in a customary display of courtesy, you immediately came to their aid with offers of food and shelter," I said with bitter cynicism.

"There was nothing I could do," he said in halfhearted defence. "The wreck happened at night, the most perilous hour for navigating around the reefs. The crew scrambled up that outcropping alongside the prow. Do you see it? It was that spot there. Naturally, they were devoured before dawn."

"Then how did you discover the Portuguese's nationality, route and destination?"

"One of them survived till morning. I don't know how, but he managed to find refuge in a tiny cabin of the prow which still lay above water. I could see his face mashed against the porthole. We couldn't understand each other at first. The glass was very thick; I could just see his lips move. Then the fellow went out on deck and we spoke for a few moments. The poor devil had gone mad, raving mad. In the end he was taken by a strange whim and fired on me with a revolver." The outline of a malicious smile crossed Gruner's face. "He mistook me for a monster. It didn't matter; the man was a lousy shot. Then he went back down into the cabin and there he stayed, waiting for night to fall. I can still recall his face, framed by the porthole. If he had had the least bit of sense the poor devil would have saved the last bullet for himself."

One could criticise Gruner for many things. It was not so much the tale itself that was cruel as the tone he used to tell it. Gruner's voice betrayed a horrifying coldness as he recounted the fate of those wretched Portuguese. He offered no personal reflections, and above all no emotions. We returned to his quarters. Gruner lectured me on the layout and defence tactics of our fortress. We were to concentrate most of our efforts on the balcony. The window slits served as both observation posts and loopholes, which controlled a 360-degree range around the lighthouse. He was not concerned about the beasts getting in through the windows. The toads would never slip through such narrow openings and the stone was too solid to break. The only way they could force an entry was through the balcony. That explained the sharpened stakes and other fortifications on the walls. Any competent marksman could defend himself against attack, no matter how intense or multitudinous.

"Essentially, the principal danger is exposing oneself on the balcony," I mused. "Why don't we simply batten down the doors with those steel shutters you fashioned?"

"In the long run it would be useless," he said. "The toads have a superhuman strength. The steel plating would slowly weaken over time and there is nothing on the island to replace it with. Shut and barred inside, I would be reduced to a prisoner of my own defences. A hole cut in the shutters wouldn't allow enough range to shoot from. No. The only solution is to keep them at bay with bullets."

After hearing him out, I had no choice but to accept his words as good sense. We made our way down to the ground floor. Three heavy wooden bars reinforced the already robust portal. They lay crosswise and could easily be pushed aside into deep openings cut for that purpose on each side of the entryway. Gruner was the mastermind behind the defences I was already familiar with outside.

"They clamber around like monkeys; it is incredible," he said with a barely contained admiration.

Gruner's last recourse had been to string up a web of empty tins and cord to signal their approach. The stones in the lighthouse wall were melded together with a paste of boiled paper mixed with sand. Nails and broken glass emerged jaggedly from those plastered fissures.

"Whatever you do, never discard a rusty nail or an empty bottle," he warned in a steely voice. "This island's currency is glass, and nails are its most precious resource."

He had little else to say. I returned to the weather official's cottage that afternoon. Compared to the lighthouse, it was a rickety and defenceless shack. Gruner had taken everything away except for my mattress. I took the mascot along with me as a precaution. It was the only way I could be sure of finding the lighthouse's door open upon my return. But Gruner gave me no cause for complaint. He seemed to accept my presence as an established fact.

I set the mattress down in a corner of the storeroom as soon as we returned to the lighthouse. That was where I would sleep, with my feet facing the ocean. The waves would swell over the rocks on stormy nights and crash against the building. Only stone separated me from the wild sea. But the lighthouse was a sturdy construction. To be at once so close to the crashing foam and yet protected from it provided the same soothing gratification as a security blanket. I had just finished setting my rather crude living quarters to rights when Gruner called from upstairs. His body emerged halfway out of the open trapdoor.

"Friend, is the door securely fastened? Come up. We are about to have company."

The living quarters were charged with an air of battle. Gruner paced about, peering through the windows, piling up ammunition, supplies and flares. All from my baggage, of course.

"What are you waiting for? Take up your rifle!" he said without looking at me. He who had once been an adversary was suddenly an ally in combat.

"How can you be certain they will attack tonight?"

"Does the Pope live in Rome?"

We positioned ourselves on the little balcony, he to the right and I on the left. The space was ridiculously narrow.

There was barely a yard separating our kneeling figures. We were surrounded by wooden spikes of varying sizes. Their points stuck out in all directions like unicorn horns. Some of them still showed traces of dried blue blood. Gruner gripped his weapon closely. A Remington and three flares lay next to him. The lighthouse's beacon was lit up. The grating of the mechanism shifted like a pendulum above us. The lens followed its course, and the noise would become deafening when the machinery creaked above our heads, only to grow fainter as it moved away. The beam swept the surrounding rock, throwing a gleaming shaft on the edges of the forest as it turned. But there was nothing there. Branches were tossed by frigid gusts of wind. It was a rasping and unrelenting sound, utterly indifferent to the uneasiness it provoked. When the lens moved off, the landscape was plunged into a near perfect darkness.

"How do we know they will head in this direction? The ocean is behind us. If they come by way of the water, they will probably scale the opposite side of the lighthouse."

"This is an island, we are surrounded by ocean. They may be beasts, but they know what doors are. Behind a door lies meat." Gruner, noticing I was still suffering from exhaustion and a bad case of nerves, said, "Go below if you wish. Load the weapons or drink rum, as you like. I have lived through enough of these attacks on my own; your presence isn't necessary."

"No, no, I can't," I answered, saying, "My fear is too great."

The tins jangled against the wall outside. "It is the wind, the wind, only the wind." He calmed me with a steadying hand. I longed to fire my weapon at something which had yet to present itself. Gruner threw a flare, twisting his head like a chameleon. The red blaze went up into the air, describing an arc as it slowly fell. A wide swath of land was bathed in crimson. But they were nowhere to be found. A second flare went up, this time green. Still nothing. The dying glow revealed only stones and trees ravaged by the wind.

"*Mein Gott, mein Gott . . .*" Gruner whispered suddenly. "There are more toads than ever."

"Where are they? I do not see a thing."

But Gruner did not answer. He might have been miles away despite being right there at my side. Gruner's mouth hung open and he drooled like a village idiot. It was as though, rather than keeping watch on the surrounding landscape, he was peering within his own soul.

"I cannot see a thing. Gruner! There is nothing there, what makes you say there are so many?"

"I can tell by the way she sings," he replied mechanically.

The mascot had begun to intone a remotely Balinese chant. It was an indescribable melody, a music that would confound any musical scale. How many human beings since the beginning of time, since the dawn of man, had suffered the privilege of hearing that music? Were Gruner and I the only ones? Or were we joined by all those who had once faced their last reckoning? It was a horrid hymn and a barbaric psalm. But its malicious innocence was beautiful, very beautiful. It played on the entire spectrum of our emotions with a surgical precision. Our feelings were confused, stirred up, and then denied three times over. The tune seemed to take on a life of its own, independent of the singer's. Nature had designed those chords to call forth the very depths of hell. The mascot sat cross-legged, as absent from the scene as Gruner was. They were far away, like those yet imperceptible monsters. One would have to be in the process of being born or dying to know the loneliness I felt that night, in the lighthouse.

"There they are," Gruner announced.

The invasion of the island had taken place at some point unseen. They emerged from the forest. Packs of monsters swarmed on both sides of the road. One could sense their presence more than see them. I could hear their voices: the sound of gargling amplified a hundred, two hundred or perhaps five hundred times over. They advanced slowly. I could begin to distinguish shapes as the gargling grew ever louder. Dear God, those deep groans made one think of someone vomiting acid. The mascot had stopped singing behind us. And for an instant it seemed as though the beasts were abandoning the lighthouse. They had been brought to a halt by the beacon's sweep. Then the mass suddenly pushed forward, a unified horde. They scurried and leaped, their heads bobbing at different heights. Inevitably, a bevy of monsters were picked out by the beam's glare as the troop advanced. I fired a scattered volley. Some shrieked and many fled, but most stayed on course. The situation called for heavy artillery. I continued to blast away frantically until Gruner seized my rifle barrel. The metal was burning hot, but the skin on his palm went unscathed.

"What the devil are you doing? Have you lost your wits? How many nights shall we hold out if you waste our ammunition so freely? We have no need for fireworks. Hold your fire until I shoot!"

I was about to receive a macabre lesson. A swarm of monsters clustered around the door. Although the beasts could not break in or scale the walls, they were able to form spontaneous towers by clambering over each other's backs. All one could see was a confused tangle of arms, legs and naked torsos. A mountain of flesh rose higher as they chaotically climbed on top of each other. Gruner held back, exhibiting a steely composure which quite horrified me. He did not take aim until their claws were practically scratching at the barricade of wooden stakes. The blast burst a monster's skull, letting fly a shrapnel-like spray of bone and brain tissue.

"Now that is how it is done!" roared Gruner. "Look to your right!"

A similar squirming pile rose beneath me. I had to shoot several beasts down before the living structure toppled. They shrieked and howled like hyenas as small bands bore the cadavers away.

"Don't fire on the deserters, it saves on bullets," Gruner advised. "When provided with enough meat, they simply devour one another."

His words proved to be correct. Each time a tower fell, the swarm of monsters resembled a crushed anthill. Packs of beasts collected the dead and left the scene. The mass soon dispersed. Constancy was not one of their virtues. As they returned to the murky deep, their parting calls sounded like a gaggle of wild geese.

"Honk, honk," Gruner mimicked disdainfully, "honk, honk! It is always the same," he said, talking as much to himself as to me. "Killing a few of them is enough to keep the rest at bay. They try to do away with good old Gruner, but they end up feasting on their own dead. Toads, vile toads."

That victory marked a turning point in our war. We still spotted two of them the following evening, although they kept their distance. Only moving shadows could be discerned on the second night. Finally, on my third night in the lighthouse, I experienced the first vigil in which not a single monster appeared. Curiously enough, it was not our most tranquil evening. Neither of us got any rest until dawn. Experience had taught Gruner that, given the toads' unpredictable nature, they were capable of attacking at any moment. "This is not a Prussian train timetable," he warned.

I had set up permanent residence on the ground floor of the lighthouse. In the evenings, I would climb the stairs to take up my watch on the balcony. As the days passed, Gruner and I settled into a curious sort of coexistence. Who was that man? He had no more vestiges of a weather official left about him as one would find in any other wizened castaway. He was egotistical and gruff as a wild cat, his lack of sociability not so much a response to his self-imposed exile as a sublimation of already existing tendencies. Despite all of his barbarity and undeniably vulgar manners, Gruner often displayed the character of a penniless aristocrat. The man was brusque, but loyal in his own way. He also possessed a lively intelligence, no matter how odd the description may sound. Gruner looked his canniest while filling his pipe. He would pack the bowl with a savage glare, keenly aware all the while of his surroundings. In those moments, he resembled an Enlightenment philosopher, putting up barriers through the sheer force of his imagination. He was the epitome of a man whose knowledge was circumscribed to a single truth, albeit a fundamental one. His was the virtue of narrowing a problem down to its essentials. Gruner was so effective at simplifying matters one could say he was capable of getting to the root of whatever matter was in question. His mind was lucid and serene whenever faced with practical concerns. He had survived thanks to an unequalled skill in that realm. Occasionally, however, his appearance would degenerate to the questionable standards of a Cossack deserter. Gruner was a supremely physical man whose hygiene left much to be desired. He munched away in true bovine fashion as he ate. His heavy breathing could be heard several yards away. He also had visionary moments, losing himself in myths of his own construction. With every gesture of disdain, Gruner made it clear that he was not made for this world; the world was made for him. The man was just like a mad Caesar, hearing the pounding hooves of invisible horses and decapitating them by the thousands.

Nevertheless, I was neither afraid of nor concerned about Gruner. It was not long before I came to expect from him a sort of twisted camaraderie. Gruner did not seem to have a treacherous nature. Who knew if it was out of intrinsic nobility or the savage veneer of rugged island life. He lived for the future – although in his case the word "future" referred strictly to "tomorrow". Once I was within the lighthouse, our coexistence was taken as a given. My very presence abolished the shared history of our pettiness, animosity and threats.

I was living through an exceptional epoch, more than willing to swallow any inconvenience in order to survive. The great difference in our characters did not bother me; I was prepared to accept that. But as in all marriages, the most insufferable dramas were brought about by the least material of concerns. For example, he utterly lacked a sense of humour. Gruner laughed only to himself, never in complicity. He would look disconcertedly at me whenever I would speak in jest, as if dimly aware that the joke was funny but not knowing why.

One morning, a light drizzle fell while the sun shone splendidly through the shower. I was reading Frazer's book, which according to Gruner belonged to the lighthouse, not to him. In other words, it must have been left behind by one of its builders. I was reading drowsily and somewhat uninterestedly when Gruner passed by. He laughed, head bowed in a futile attempt to contain himself. I will never know if he was trying to tell me something or merely happened to be wandering by. He laughed and laughed, punctuating it with an odd punchline from a half-told joke:

". . . he wasn't a sodomite, he was an Italian."

It was a cavernous and infectious chortle. Gruner repeated, "He wasn't a sodomite, he was an Italian." As he climbed the stairs, he laughed and retold the end of that mysterious anecdote.

The next time I heard him laugh was another matter

entirely. I had just retired to my mattress after a particularly violent attack. The danger had passed; it was growing light out. I was settling down to sleep when a series of noises pulled me from my bed. The little beast was moaning. Was he beating her? No. The mascot was soon drowned out by a lustful Gruner. I could not believe my ears, and wondered if I might not be hallucinating. No, no, I was not. They were most certainly moans of pleasure. The bed upstairs banged rhythmically against the bare wooden planks dividing from their sport. Minute wood shavings began to drift down, as if it were snowing inside the lighthouse. My head and shoulders were soon sprinkled with those flakes of wood. The lighthouse's circular form magnified and echoed every noise as my imagination envisaged the scene above with incredulity. The fornication continued for an hour or two until it was brought to an abrupt halt by a crescendo of grunts and thrusts.

How could he lie with one of the very same monsters that plagued us every night? How did he manage to justify the act, in defiance of all the obstacles set down by civilisation and nature? It was worse than cannibalism, which is almost understandable under desperate circumstances. Gruner's sexual incontinence was worthy of a clinical study.

Naturally, discretion and good manners did not allow me to comment on Gruner's zoophilia. At the same time, it was obvious that I knew. He failed to mention it out of carelessness, not shame. It was Gruner himself who brought the matter up one day in passing. Without showing excessive interest or disdain, I posed a question of a practical nature:

"Does she suffer from dyspareunia?"

"Disparoon . . . what?"

"Dyspareunia, painful copulation."

We were eating at the table and his mouth was opened wide for a bite, the spoon poised in midair. Gruner never finished his meal. He laughed so hard I thought his lower jaw would come unhinged. His guffaws welled up from his belly, chest and neck. The man almost lost his balance from slapping his legs so. Shedding great big tears, he paused to wipe them away and resumed his cackling. Gruner laughed and laughed; he began to polish a rifle but could not stop snickering. His hilarity did not let up until it grew dark and the night demanded our undivided attention.

However, when the topic of the mascot happened to come up again and I enquired why she wore that absurd scarecrow outfit, that dirty, stretched-out and fraying jersey, the answer was as emphatic as it was final:

"For decency's sake."

That was the way of the man.

# 7

The Japanese philosopher Musashi once said that only a select few appreciate the art of war. Gruner is one of them. The battle is defensive at night. Amorous forays with the mascot fill his days. It is hard to tell which of the two activities impassions him most. Gruner discovered a pair of wolf traps among my supplies. The irons are as cruel as shark jaws. He set out the snares well within range of our bullets. The assault last night was comparatively mild. Two monsters were captured, three killed. These casualties were strictly unnecessary if we are to follow Gruner's doctrine of conserving resources. He went to inspect the snares in the morning, driven by an unspeakable desire for battle trophies. The monsters, in their craving for meat, had already taken the cadavers away and the snared monsters with them. The loss frustrated him greatly.

JANUARY 13

To continue on with Musashi: A good warrior is not defined by the cause he defends, but rather by the meaning he derives from the struggle. Sadly, this aphorism is meaningless at the lighthouse.

**JANUARY 14**

Early evening: the sky is unusually free of clouds. There is an impressive array of fixed and shooting stars. The sight brings tears to my eyes. My thoughts dwell on the latitude and the positioning of the firmament. I am so far from home that the constellations have come unhinged from their usual positions and I am unable to recognise them. But we must accept that there is no such thing as chaos. It is simply the human incapacity to assimilate new arrangements and orderings in the world. The universe is not susceptible to chaos; we are.

**JANUARY 16**

Nothing. No attack.

**JANUARY 17**

Nothing.

**JANUARY 18**

Nothing, nothing at all. Where have they gone?

**JANUARY 19–25**

The austral summer is fading timidly, but with grandeur. I spotted a butterfly today. Here, inside the lighthouse. It flitted by, indifferent to our torment. Gruner made a halfhearted attempt to crush it in his palm. It would have been a shame. The cold is encroaching and I doubt we shall see another. But it would be impossible to express such a sentiment to a man like him.

This leads me to a more disquieting and less wistful reflection. The summer nights were exceedingly short. Now we are inexorably heading toward the winter, or rather the darkness. The monsters always swarm at night. Their strikes grow ever longer. How will it be when the nights last twenty hours or more?

**JANUARY 26**

Due to the reduced dimensions of the island, objects tend to erode beneath our gaze. My eyes have scrutinised every surface a thousand times. We speak of the lighthouse and its environs as if it were an entire state. Every nook and cranny has a name; every tree, every stone. An oddly shaped branch is baptised immediately. Distances are distended out of proportion. To hear us speak, anyone would think we were referring to remote places. Actually, everything is within walking distance.

Time also becomes relative. A drop of water may suspend from a spiderweb for centuries before it falls. But then again, a week passes in the blink of an eye.

## JANUARY 27

Thanks to the lighthouse's peculiar acoustics, I cannot help overhearing erotic murmurings. Gruner generally sets to his pleasure at the first glimpses of dawn, once I have gone downstairs. He can draw out the activity for two, three or even four hours. His moans occur with clockwork regularity. He sounds like a thirsty man crossing the desert, in the throes of a monotonous agony. I sometimes think he could lose himself in that syncopated rhythm for days on end.

The mascot is curiously insatiable. One can chart the progress of her perpetual arousal, from the accelerating spasms to the culminating climax that finishes the job. The effervescent explosion of volcanic and long-drawn-out squeals occurs every one and a half minutes. This acute ecstasy is sustained for twenty full seconds, and far from ending, the whole process begins again. Gruner pounds the beast over and over with complete indifference until he consummates his pleasure with a low oath.

## JANUARY 28

Crabs form a part of our diet. They would be considered inedible in Europe. Their shells are extremely thick, beneath which there is a great deal of fat and precious little meat. But we have no other choice than to accept them gladly. At first, I leapt like an ingenuous fool among the rocks on the coast. The crabs skittered down into the crevices, evading me with ease. The waves splashed hollowly against the crags, dousing me with the spray. The whole endeavour was not so much diverting as it was perilous. I had merely intended to enliven the lighthouse's stores, but my fingers had grown stiff in the icy water. I was unused to such small but constant hardships.

Luckily, Gruner happened by, commenting, "Friend, you look like a lame goat."

He was heading for the forest with a hatchet swung over his shoulder. The mascot followed close behind. He called out a command with a smack of his lips. The beast slithered between the stones like a snake, snatching up the crabs with insulting ease. She also collected a species of mussel, which adhered so firmly to the stones that I had not even considered removing them. The job clearly seemed to require both a scalpel and a hammer. The mascot made do with her fingernails. I was relegated to holding the basket open for the beast. The mascot would occasionally rip off a crab's leg and swallow it whole before throwing the rest of it in with the others.

I discovered an edible mushroom in the forest, my sole contribution to our diet. It clings to tree roots with the same tenacity as the crustaceans adhere to the rocks. One must extricate them with a knife. The fungi are sure to be of little nutritional value, but I gather them anyway. I also crush the roots of various sylvan plants, reducing them to a vitamin paste.

As Gruner is such a reticent and silent man, I feel compelled to register one of our more voluble exchanges.

"And how do you know the herbs are not poisonous?" he asked, looking doubtfully at a syrup concocted from mixing the paste with gin.

"Herbs are like people. Each one possesses unique characteristics. They cannot be labelled simply as medicinal or poisonous," I answered, taking a swig. "It is a question of knowing what one is dealing with, that is all."

"The world is filled with horrid people, very horrid. One should have to be a perfect child to trust in human kindness."

"The inherent moral worth of an individual is irrelevant. The question is whether people, once thrown together, are able to form a functioning society. The balance of a man's worth does not depend on inclinations of character. Imagine a pair of castaways, two exceedingly detestable characters. Separately, they may be odious. But once at each other's mercy, they would opt for the only possible solution: unite in order to create the best living conditions possible. What would their personal failings matter?"

But I couldn't be sure he was listening. Gruner gulped the swill down and said, "We drink schnapps in Austria. I prefer gin."

Gruner and I also fish. He had long since placed a complete array of rods along the southern coast before my arrival. They were driven into the rock fissures, like slender staffs projecting out into the open sea. Contrary to what one might think, our problem was not so much the meagreness as the overabundance of our catch. The fish at these latitudes are either truly dimwitted or they simply have never seen a hook before. Their combined bulk and vigour, however, is enough to snap a rod in two. To forestall this problem, Gruner thrust the poles firmly into the crevices. He fashioned snares out of steel wire with hooks shaped like chicken feet. Despite all his efforts, a fishing rod gets lost now and then. One can still see them tossing in the currents a full day after having been rent from their moorings. We burst into impotent rage upon discovering such losses. Still, one must admit that the island sustains us. The provisions I brought with me complement and enliven our meals, but our survival does not depend on them.

## JANUARY 29

My daily routine: I abandon my post on the balcony at the break of dawn. After having removed my rifle, I stretch out on the mattress, often still fully dressed. I lose consciousness like an oil lamp being snuffed out. Nature dictates the length of my slumber. I lost the ability to recall my dreams upon entering the lighthouse.

I generally wake at midday, or thereabouts. I breakfast on a tin plate, like a prisoner. If the weather is exceptionally fine, I may take the plate outside. I see to my toilette once back inside. This is the highlight of my day. But it seems that my hair or at least those locks on the nape of my neck have changed colour permanently. They turned ash grey during those first days of terror and remain so still. My wardrobe is quite simple. The trousers I wear most often are made from a coarse cloth, ideally suited for rough labour. A sailor's high-necked sweater tops several layers of undershirts.

I do callisthenics twice a week even if it rains, as it often does. For want of a barber in these remote climes, I hack off my own hair in the style of a medieval page. But I am quite scrupulous about shaving. Why do I so love the feel of perfectly smooth cheeks? Sometimes the distinction between barbarity and civilisation is dependent on such an insignificant thing as a good shave. Gruner's unruly beard disgusts me. He takes very little care of it. One would think that he went at it with a hatchet. It is far worse when he sunbathes outside, with his back leaning against the lighthouse wall. Gruner adopts a crocodile-like stillness while the mascot agilely runs her fingers through his beard. I finally realised one day why she did so. It was to feast on the morsels lodged in his tangle.

The rest of the day is given over to a series of chores, which Gruner and I have divided between us. I collect firewood. The logs take time to dry and must be piled in the shelter of the lighthouse long before they may be burned. In the end, the work may be useless, but it gives us an illusion, however false, of the future. I gather and store the fishing rods, repair and reinforce the network of tins, smash bottles and search for rusty nails to make the cracks in the stone even more deadly. It is inconceivable to someone outside the lighthouse how a scant quarter of an inch of bare space between one key and another or between two shards of glass may become an obsession. I also carve fresh stakes of wood, keep track of our dwindling supply of ammunition, and ration the food supplies. Gruner does not argue with my schemes as a general rule. For example, I proposed that we incise a star into the base of an ordinary bullet cartridge, transforming it into a fragmentary shell. I also suggested that we insert short, sharp stakes into the natural fissures of rock around the lighthouse so that the monsters would injure the soles of their feet as they surged forward. The idea came straight out of Roman military strategy. It obviously does not keep them from drawing near, but it certainly makes it more difficult. Indeed, this innovation has cast a lugubrious pallor over our surroundings.

I dispose of leisure time until nightfall, if such a concept means anything here at the lighthouse.

**FEBRUARY 1**

A lovely evening. The horizon resembled a colossal stage-set as day drew to a close; the light was sucked away, beaten down and overlaid with washes of ink. It was as though a giant brush had painted the sky black, letting the minute sparks of stars shine through. While on watch, I noticed we were being spied on by an unusually small and early-rising monster. The beast was so well hidden I shouldn't have spotted him. But the little creature happened to be perched in the very tree where I had unsuccessfully attempted to murder Gruner. He observed me like a two-armed mollusc. I was sitting on a stool, smoking. I set the cigarette on the railing and calmly took aim. The monster did not associate my posture with imminent death. He remained in the tree, gazing at me in puzzlement. His heart was set squarely in my line of fire. A shot rang out. The monster toppled, pulling a jumble of leaves down along with him. I lost sight of the thing for an instant. But his legs got caught up in branches before hitting the ground. The monster's arms dangled loosely; he was dead. The bullet had gone straight through his chest.

Gruner chided me about the wasted bullet. I reminded him of the traps he had set. Was it really necessary to fire on immobilised and thus harmless creatures?

"We must be thrifty," says he. "Ammunition is life."

"I am the one who brought the ammunition," I reply, "and I shall use it as I see fit."

We quarrelled through the wee hours like two children.

**FEBRUARY 2**

The monsters spent this entire night howling out in the darkness without attacking; very curious indeed. I made an unsuccessful attempt to draw Gruner into a conversation about our past lives in Europe.

It is impossible to establish the slightest camaraderie with this man. It is not so much that he refuses to speak, or conceals anything from me. He is completely indifferent to banal, everyday conversation. If I talk about myself, he nods his head. When I ask about his life, Gruner responds in monosyllables, ever vigilant to the encroaching darkness outside. This pattern continues until I grow weary of the pantomime. Imagine two men slumbering side by side, talking in their sleep. That is the exact nature of our dialogues.

**FEBRUARY 5–20**

Nothing. This nothingness is accompanied by the mascot's silence. It is a good sign when she ceases her song. I scarcely have any contact with her. The mascot is either fornicating with Gruner, occupied with simple tasks, or avoiding me. She begrudges our first encounter with the long memory of a beaten dog. Our paths inevitably cross when she goes to and from the lighthouse. The little beast quickens her step and keeps at a safe distance, like a little sparrow.

At times the mere sight of the mascot gives me shudders. One may deduce from a cursory observation that she is a quadruped; thermostatic, colour-blind, bilious and spineless. Nevertheless, the mascot's form and mannerisms are so human that it requires a great effort not to exchange

pleasantries with her. At least until one is confronted with
the brainpower of a chicken. She is incapable of looking,
listening, seeing or even hearing us. The mascot inhabits
another sphere, and this separation is what she and Gruner
have in common.

## FEBRUARY 22

Gruner has got drunk. This is quite an uncommon occur-
rence. I saw he was inebriated, a bottle of gin in one hand
and a rifle in the other, thrashing about like a witch doctor
on the lighthouse's craggy foundations. Then he melted into
the forest, only to return with the last light. Meanwhile, I
captured the mascot and carried her into a corner after a
heated struggle. She was deathly afraid, unaware that I
merely intended to examine her skull. The mascot's head is
perfect. I am referring to the cranium's uniform smoothness;
a spherical form free of any abrasion. Hers is a splendidly
rounded arch, whereas humans' tend to be riddled with
bumps and bulges. Is it shaped this way in order to withstand the water pressure of the deep? The cranium exhibits
neither the indentations of a born criminal nor the protu-
berances of a prodigy. Phrenologists would be surprised to
learn that there is absolutely no pronounced development
of the parietal or occipital lobes. The overall volume of the
head is slightly smaller than that of a Slavic female and is
dilated six per cent more than a Breton goat's. I took hold

of the mascot's cheeks, and forced her mouth open. In place of tonsils was a second palate, which surely serves to impede the entry of water. The monster appears to lack a sense of smell, clinically known as anosmia. On the other hand, her tiny ears have a canine ability to distinguish sounds that are inaudible to humans. The mascot has frequent bouts of dreaminess during which her attention is taken up by untold voices, melodies or incantations. What does she hear in those moments? It is impossible to tell. The webbing on her hands is not as wide or as long as the male monsters'. She can separate her first two fingers at an angle unthinkable in human anatomy. My hypothesis is that this flexion helps propel the monsters underwater. I practically had to tear the clothing off her, she struggled so. The monster's physique is of an admirable architecture. European girls would pale at the sight of her form. A pair of silk gloves is all that is needed to make her a model fit for the salons of Paris.

As weather official, I can attest that this island is situated in a peculiar maritime region, surrounded by warm-water currents. That would explain everything, from the abundance of vegetation to the absence of snow, which should have fallen by now. Perhaps even the presence of these beasts in the environs may be attributed to these unique conditions. There would have been some record of the monsters' existence, apart from legend, if they had proliferated in other waters. I once read that the blood of polar fish contains a substance which prevents freezing. I fancy the beasts share this trait, given their blue blood. Otherwise, how might such complex organisms inhabit frigid waters and yet lack layers of accumulated fat? Her marblelike musculature is sheathed in a taut skin tinged in exquisite varnishes of salamander green. Imagine a wood nymph with a serpent's skin. Her nipples are little black buttons. The creature's breasts seemed to be held up by invisible strings. Here one must refer to the French gold standard: a perfect breast must nestle comfortably in a champagne glass. Her overall muscle tone displays health and vitality; no need for a girdle. Ballerina hips and a flat, flat stomach. Thighs as solid as the rock beneath us. The texture of her face is consistent with the rest of her skin, whereas human flesh often manifests distinct contradictions between cheek and thigh. The mascot is enveloped in a minutely pored membrane. There are no hair follicles on her head, armpits or pubis. No sculptor would be able to replicate how perfectly such miraculously lithe buttocks join her thighs. Her profile is distinctly Egyptian. A tapered nose contrasts sharply with her spherical skull and doelike eyes. The forehead rises gently like a sweet, sweet cliff, finer than any found on a Roman bust.

The dumb beast trembled with fear as I took her off into a corner, just as a cow is incapable of understanding the rationale behind a veterinarian's poking and prodding. I lit a candle and waved it to and fro before her eyes. The pupils contracted, becoming tiny feline slits in the glaring light. I could not help shuddering as I observed her. The eyes were vibrant blue mirrors; more round than oval. They glinted like amber. The ocular fluid had the density of mercury. I saw myself within those orbs, gazing at her. That is to say, gazing at myself. I almost broke off the investigation. I was overcome by a bout of absurd vertigo on seeing my reflection in the eyes of a monster. May only those who have suffered the same be my judge.

It is impossible to keep my distance while studying the mascot. One touch and I am ensnared. I press my palm to her cheek and pull my hand away in horror, as if electrocuted. The association between human contact and warmth is one of our most primal instincts. There are no cold bodies, at least not living ones. I am at once attracted and repelled by her temperature. It is reminiscent of a cadaver, freshly dead.

**FEBRUARY 25**

They have finally appeared, and in great numbers. Our daily ration of ammunition is six bullets and we were forced to fire eight.

**FEBRUARY 26**

Between the two of us, Gruner and I have spent nineteen bullets.

**FEBRUARY 27**

Thirty-three.

**FEBRUARY 28**

Thirty-seven.

**MARCH 1–16**

My struggle for survival has kept me from writing. At any rate, nothing that I might record bears remembrance.

**MARCH 18**

The assaults are not quite as fierce as before. I spent a long while observing the lighthouse and the balcony from the forest's interior. Gruner was intrigued by my vigil and joined me without uttering a word. Our shoulders grazed as we stood side by side. I was curious to examine the lighthouse from the monsters' point of view. My intention was to descend into the gloom of their bloodthirsty minds and imagine how our fortification must look to them.

Gruner, after a certain space of time, intoned: "Well, I for one fail to see any weakness in our defences." And he strode off.

**MARCH 20–21**

The monsters have taken to watching us without attacking. This was disquieting at first, then merely curious. We usually catch fleeting glimpses of their forms. They may occasionally be seen among the trees or in the shallows about the reefs. They vanish when caught in the beam's glare.

Darkness encroaches on our days. Now we have just three hours of solar light left to us. Even as the sun rises, it is beginning to set. Life on the island would be a formidable and taxing experience under any circumstances. However, being besieged by monsters surpasses the bounds of human understanding. Although it may seem strange, the lulls between fighting are often worse than the battles themselves. We listen to the muddled chorus of wind, rain and sea as we wait for a new day in the dim glow of the oil lamps, ignorant as to what shall greet us first, light or death. Never should I have thought to find hell in such a simple thing as a clock without hands.

**THE IDES OF MARCH**

I have discovered that Gruner knows how to play chess. This rather insignificant fact is an oasis of civilisation in the midst of all this madness. Three games. Two stalemates and one checkmate. Need one mention who claimed himself victorious?

**APRIL 4**

The assaults swept over us in six successive waves tonight. My rifle lock was burning from overuse. I had no choice. Gruner voiced no complaints concerning wasted ammunition.

**APRIL 8**

I practice complex opening manoeuvres in an attempt to topple Gruner's defences. Gruner is particularly shrewd in that way. He rooks me, and wears down my offensives, piece by piece. The similarities between his personality and chess game are too obvious to mention. Either way, the Grunertian or Gruneristic mentality made its presence felt.

The monsters could be heard crying out in the darkness, beyond the reach of the lighthouse beam. They sounded a bit like vultures squabbling over carrion. Then they surged forward abruptly, but skittered away before we could take aim. It is all such an enigma. The worst of it is that the monsters' actions are completely devoid of logic. This makes them utterly unpredictable.

**APRIL 10–22**

I have been meditating on my reasons for coming to this island. I had been seeking peace in nothingness. And in place of silence I have found a monster-plagued inferno. What revelations have been hidden from my sight? Although I rack my brain for answers, all else pales before this evidence: monsters, monsters and more monsters. There is nothing else to judge or consider.

**APRIL 23 AND 24**

Horrific combat, man against beast. Shooting at such close quarters has adorned the balustrade with viscera, grey matter and blue blood. The monsters climbed so high up the stakes these past two nights that we resorted to kicks, stabs and swings of the hatchet in order to ward them off. Gruner is at his most savage in these moments. Gruner threw his rifle aside with a battle cry just as the monsters had got perilously close and the last line of stakes had begun to give way under the mass of arms and legs. I kept up a steady stream of bullets several steps behind. He grasped the harpoon in one hand and the hatchet in the other. The man wounded, mutilated and killed with chaotic frenzy, his limbs transformed into a deadly windmill. Gruner was an authentic demon, a desperate Viking, the marauding pirate Red Beard; all this and more. The sight made me shudder and I should not fancy him for an enemy. I witnessed these images myself not hours ago, and yet I experienced them as though under the effects of some hallucinogen. I have grave doubts as to my mental health in the light of day. Our life in the lighthouse is so far-fetched.

**MAY 2**

I discern some slight twinges of appreciation in Gruner. This is never expressed explicitly. Not one kind word falls from his lips. Nevertheless, he is aware of how my presence contributes to his survival. Gruner confessed that the attacks of late are beyond anything he has experienced before. A lone man would never be able to defend himself against this swarm of insects escaped from a hellish insane asylum. Not even him.

But we cannot go on in this way. One of these days we shall be outnumbered.

**MAY 5**

No change. Gruner is a cipher. There is a great contrast between the dangers that threaten us and his ever-altering moods. He appears to pass his days with increasing contentment as our nights become ever more taxing. The euphoria of battle has taken hold of him; a longing for the abyss. He cannot accept that we are not playing chess and that it would take just one loss to seal our doom.

**MAY 6**

One of Gruner's bullets grazed me this evening. It slashed my sleeve, leaving a superficial wound. But he had saved me from an overwhelming monster. I was left with no choice but to justify the wound and praise him.

**MAY 11**

The assaults are ever more savage. Some of the monsters managed to scale the opposite wall of the lighthouse and attack us from above, where the barricade of stakes is weakest. They were literally falling out of the sky. Our rifle barrels flew up and down in an attempt to control the teeming beasts below. We fire an average of fifty bullets every night. The sheer quantity of monsters exceeds our worst nightmares.

Today's vigil ended in a bitter discussion. Gruner accused me of not having kept the fortification of nails and glass shards in good repair. He blamed me for letting his "toads" slither up the walls. Beside myself, I denied it vehemently. I work on that grim mosaic twice as much as he does, if only out of boredom. Insults were exchanged. I told him that he was nothing more than a base fornicator and a surly one at that. Gruner cut me short by reminding me that I was merely a blasted intruder. He had never uttered that word before. We are deeper in the pit than ever.

**MAY 12**

A monster sank his teeth into Gruner's right foot. I fired immediately, but its jaws tore away Gruner's boot and a chunk of his big toe along with it. He treated the wound without a whimper.

But we will not be able to hold out for much longer.

# 8

The escalation of the monsters' fury was wearing us down slowly but surely. We were like two mountain climbers trying to scale great heights with not enough oxygen. Our actions were mechanical. If we spoke, it was with the weariness of mediocre actors reciting a lacklustre script. This fatigue was quite distinct from that which I experienced in the very first days. It was a less palpable form of lingering exhaustion; less desperate, but ever so much rawer. We no longer spoke. Like two condemned men awaiting execution, we had nothing left to say to one another. The only words that escaped Gruner's lips for days on end were "friend", if he needed something urgently, or the warning *"Zum Leuchtturm"*, reserved for the wee hours of night.

Here is an example of a typical scene from this period: I am already awake and have completed some task deemed indispensable for our safety. I climb up to the light tower for lack of any other occupation. This is the highest point on the island, and one can see clear to the edges of the horizon. I am there in the hope of spying a lost ship. None appears.

A simple iron weathervane crowns the lighthouse's pointed roof. Although out of sight, I can hear it creaking languidly. It makes no difference in what direction it is pointing.

The island is bathed in a dense pink light just after midday, which accentuates the minuteness of this island, in the middle of such a melancholy ocean. The treetops shimmer with matte glimmerings. The land lacks not just physical heat but the warmth of human activity. There is not a single bird to be seen. A clump of greenery dips into the water on the southern coast. A curtain of branches and leaves meets the ocean as though it were on the banks of a tropical river. It is an incongruous sight. If I look a bit farther, I can see my first residence. It is scarcely a thousand metres away. But one could say that an entire epoch lies between me and that cottage. Now I can only view it from a military standpoint. It is abandoned territory.

I am on the balcony. Gruner is below me; walking. Or, I should say, scuttling. It is difficult to credit the endless quantity of things he finds to occupy himself with here at the lighthouse. He always busies himself with some activity, despite his weak flesh and frigid soul. When Gruner isn't sleeping, fornicating or fighting, he is taken up in the most obscure minutiae. For example, he is capable of sharpening a key with a jeweller's fastidiousness for hours on end. Or he splays himself out in the sun, eyes closed and chest bared. If Gruner opened his mouth, he would look just like a crocodile. Nothing else matters to him. "We are going to die," I said one day. "It is only death, after all," he answered with a Bedouin's fatalism. He occasionally sits down on a rock and does nothing but stare off into the middle distance. It is revealing precisely because there is nothing revealing about it. His gaze is that of a sleepwalker's as he attempts to elude time's grasp. He is oblivious to everything as he stares ahead, even the little stakes protruding menacingly out of the rock crevices. His body seems to become a pagan totem as it merges with the stone. Gruner lives in a state of perpetual death. A monotonous alarm sounds when evening falls:

"*Zum Leuchtturm!* The lighthouse!"

Our apathy came to an end one day when, by chance, Gruner went up to the lens room. While he was checking to make sure that the lights were in working order, I gazed off in the direction of the small Portuguese boat. Gruner's hands were fumbling with the machinery. For want of anything else to say, I asked him what the ship had been carrying.

"Explosives," he said as he got down on his knees to adjust the angle of the lenses.

"Are you positive?" I asked without much conviction, not much interested in the answer.

"Dynamite, contraband dynamite," he replied with customary bluntness.

The conversation ended there. Later, I was able to piece together more information concerning the explosives. According to the sailor who survived, the ship was smuggling illegal dynamite. They had obtained it from the surplus stock of South African miners for a mere pittance and were planning to resell it for an astronomical price in Chile or Argentina, where it would have served the cause of some obscure revolution. I had noticed a complete deep-sea diver's suit in the lighthouse. It was several days before the idea took hold in my mind. I grew giddy just thinking about it. That night was horrific. The beasts pummelled the door. Bullet after bullet flew from Gruner's gun out into the darkness, but our defences were weakening. Gruner sent me downstairs to reinforce the door. The howls resonated against the lighthouse's walls like a massive organ as I descended the stairs. I very nearly turned back. And yet somehow I managed to reach that portal. For all of its solidity, the iron was beginning to buckle. The wooden bars were cracked and creaked with each heave. There was really very little I could do. If they forced their way in, we would be devoured by the mass; we would be dead men. But they gave up, perhaps because Gruner had killed enough of them, or perhaps they had simply grown weary of battle.

The next morning, Gruner requested my council. I assented out of curiosity. It was completely out of character for him to take such an initiative.

"After dinner," he said.

"After dinner," I confirmed. And then he disappeared. I imagine he secreted himself somewhere in the forest. Gruner must have been very distressed in order to give himself over to solitary reflection.

I set to reinforcing the network of rope and cowbells garlanding the lighthouse. Gruner had neglected to put that horrid jersey back on the little beast after having his way with her. She was nude and unaware of my presence. The mascot was heading toward a thin strip of sand bounded by the tallest and sharpest rocks on the coast. Weary of my task, I followed her.

I drew closer, leaping across the high, craggy reefs which jutted out from that section of the coast. There were so many of them. Those promontories often reminded me of the mouth of a sleeping giant, nestled underground. His teeth were rocks, and his gums were made of sand. Little coves caught the winds between the outcroppings. I looked about and found the mascot in one of those cavities. Her body was splayed out like a lizard's. The beast was so still she could easily have been confused with the surrounding rock. The waves swept in, occasionally engulfing her form. But she was as indifferent to water as a shellfish. The beast ignored the tides just as she ignored me. I was perched on a rock right above her. She must have been aware of my presence.

Seeing her thus, one could understand how Gruner had

given in to carnal instinct. This time, my curiosity was no longer of a scientific nature. She must have grasped this in some way, as she did not flee; nor was she frightened. I ran my fingers down her spine. Her damp skin was slick, as if coated in oil. The mascot did not move. It disturbed me that this touch did not seem to have any effect on her. A wave crashed, covering her in its foam and forming a scrim about her body. I was at once tempted and shamed by the white frothy curtain. I slunk off, deeply indignant with myself. I felt as if I had been insulted by an anonymous and incontestable voice.

Gruner did indeed speak to me after dinner. We left the lighthouse on the pretense of taking the air. It was a testament as opposed to a talk. We walked through the forest, and without making any direct reference to defeat or abandoning his plebian stoicism, he described the situation in this manner:

"Leave if you wish. Perhaps you are not aware that we possess a dinghy. It was left here by the ship which dropped me off on the island. It can be found on a small beach adjacent to the weather official's house, but a bit to the north. The boat is concealed in the undergrowth. It has been quite some time since I have gone near, but I doubt that the toads have harmed it in any way. The only human thing they care for is flesh. You may take all the provisions and potable water the craft will hold."

He paused to light a cigarette. This was followed by a series of expansive gesticulations involving his arms, mouth and tobacco in an attempt to express his utter contempt for the future.

"Obviously, it will be of no use. There is no landmass within reach and you shan't encounter any ships. You shall perish from thirst and hunger. That is if a storm does not wreck the flimsy shell first. Or the toads do not overtake it. But I shall not deny you the right to choose."

I lit a cigarette rather than answer him and stood rooted to the ground before him. The air was unusually cold. Clouds of vapour escaped from our mouths, mingling with the tobacco smoke. Although Gruner saw that I was ruminating, he could but little imagine the direction that my thoughts had taken.

"I believe we should assume more risks," I declared at last. "As things stand, we have nothing to lose. Nothing will stop the monsters if they manage to break the door down. I noticed we have a set of deep-sea diver's equipment with an air pump. Do you think we would be able to haul the lot to the dinghy and then row it up to the Portuguese vessel?"

Gruner was at a loss. He knitted his eyebrows.

"The dynamite, the dynamite," I said, pointing to the ship with a cigarette dangling from my outstretched hand. Gruner's whole body stiffened as if coming to military attention.

"Hear me out, Gruner, it may not be as suicidal as it seems. The monsters are no different from any other predator, they only attack at night. That means they rest during the day. We shall have every chance of success if we time our exhibition carefully. And the ocean is immense. Who can tell where they dwell? Who knows, their lair may be on the other side of the island or ten yards off the coast. As you said yourself, there is nothing of interest for them there; they have no reason to go near."

Gruner shook his head as though it were all nonsense. I refused to give way.

"Let me tell you a story!" bellowed Gruner. "There was once a poor lad, a farm boy. He hid himself up in the trees and under furniture. Whenever he came out of hiding, he was met with fists. End of story."

"I need you. Someone must man the air pump. I shan't be able to manage it alone."

Up until then, he had been listening to me with the same patience one might devote to a backward child or a doddering elder. He turned his back to me as I continued my tirade.

"Wait!" I exclaimed, grasping his sleeve.

Gruner jerked his arm away with unexpected violence and muttered several German oaths unknown to Goethe's pen. He walked away, still mumbling darkly. I followed him at a distance. Once back at the lighthouse, Gruner set to work repairing the door. He ignored my presence completely as he went about his task. His efforts might forestall the final outcome, but they could never avoid it.

"Think of your rooks, Gruner," I said to him. "A king is nothing without the defence of a tower." Then I brought my lips to his ear and whispered as if at a confession box: "One hundred dead. Two hundred, three hundred monsters destroyed by a single bomb. Gruner, it shall give them an unforgettable lesson, one that will save our lives. All depends on you." I had made my case. And it seemed wise to give him time to mull it over. Naturally, I was fully aware of the recklessness of my proposal. But the alternatives were far worse. Set off in the dinghy? Where could I go? Withstand their attacks? For how long? Gruner viewed our plight from the perspective of a fanatic and stubborn warrior. I laboured with the desperation of a gambler who has just bet his last coin at the casino, as it would be pointless to save it.

I gathered a load of tools, rags mummified by the cold, kerosene jugs and empty sacks. I wanted to find the dinghy Gruner had mentioned, check its condition and, if need be, caulk it. Then I would stop by the weather official's cottage to collect more nails and, above all, hinges. They would certainly come in handy at the lighthouse. I was carrying a heavy load when the mascot crossed my path. I shifted the greater part of the burden onto her back and indicated our route with a rough shove.

Indeed, the boat was exactly where Gruner had indicated. It was a small cove, camouflaged by trees and clumps of moss which clung to the wood like a skin disease. The dinghy's interior was flooded. But a cursory inspection revealed that the source of the water was rain, not leaks. It did not take much effort to empty the little boat and remove the encrusted vegetation.

Thus, all was in readiness for my expedition. The only hurdle remaining was that Gruner should accompany me and agree to commit a valiant suicide. My mind was already made up. A rare calmness of spirit came over me. The cove was shaped like a horseshoe and no larger than a small stable. It shut off the horizon; the open sea was barely visible. I watched how the waves jostled fitfully against the boat's sides. Although we would surely die, it would be the death we had chosen. It might be considered a privilege under the circumstances. I stood calmly on the beach for quite a while. I did nothing more than clean my nails. I reflected on my past as the manicure progressed.

Life is but a small thing. However, humans have acquired the rather tiring habit of brooding on their fleeting passage through the world. My first childhood memory and my last glimpse of civilisation filled my mind's eye. The first thing I remembered was a port. I was perhaps three years old, or thereabouts. I was seated on a high chair with dozens of other children alongside. But out the window I could see the dreariest quay in the world. My last memory was also of docks. That was all one could see from the ship that carried me away from Europe to the island. Yes, life is but a small thing.

The mascot was seated on a throne of moss, hands grasping at her crossed ankles as she leaned against the wall of tree trunks. Her eyes were lost in some nonexistent infinitude. It made such a natural and fitting scene that my eyes were pained by her pauper's rags. But let us not play innocent: I already knew what I wanted even before removing that ripped jersey. I was close to death. When one is faced with mortality, such ethical quibbles are but dust in the road. I would most surely die, and the mascot was the closest thing resembling a woman within my reach. I was going to perish, and hearing the moans and sighs emitting from that body, day after day, had made me indifferent to moral scruples.

What took place, however, was most unexpected. I had foreseen a brief copulation, sullied and brusque. Instead, I entered within an oasis. At first, the coldness of her skin sent me a-shivering. But our temperatures calibrated themselves to some unheard-of degree in which such concepts as hot and cold became meaningless. Her body was a living sponge spilling forth opium. My humanity was annulled. Oh Lord, how wonderful it was! All women, whether honest or of ill repute, were but lackeys in a court they should never enter, apprentices of a guild that had yet to be founded. Did her touch unlock a mystic portal? No. It was quite the opposite. A grotesque truth was revealed to me, at once transcendent and puerile, as I fornicated with that nameless mascot. Europe had no idea that it was living in a state of perpetual castration. Her sexuality was free from every encumbrance. One could not even say she possessed any particular amorous skill. The monster simply fornicated, throwing her every muscle into copulation. In those moments there was neither tenderness nor sweetness; no rancour or pain. There was neither the price of a whorehouse nor the offering of a lover. That act reduced our bodies to their most elemental, basic state. The more bestial our exertions, the greater her delight. I felt an exclusively physical pleasure, the like of which I had never known.

A man of my age and relative experience, regardless of his origins, has inevitably felt his measure of both love and hate. He has had his moments of sadness and grasped at snatches of beauty. But it is not always a man's lot to know extreme passion. For however much they may long for desire, suspecting that it must exist somewhere, millions of men have lived and died, and shall live and die, without discovering this faculty, which came so simply and naturally to her. Until that moment, my body had obtained gratification as any good bourgeois might deposit capital. She had given me an awareness of my body. The beast destroyed every link between my person and my pleasure, as though lust itself were a living thing. When the moment of climax came, I was beyond ecstasy; I had reached the zenith of human experience.

Everything must come to an end, even that. I slowly came back into myself, blinking my eyes as if to hasten the transition back to normalcy. It took me several minutes to regain the temperature, smells and colours of my surroundings. The beast did not move from her mossy cushion. She gazed up at the sky and stretched her arms languidly. What is so wrong about it, I asked, not knowing quite what the question meant nor quite why I was asking it. Once back to my old self, or someone at any rate, I was overwhelmed by a vague sensation of ridiculousness. I felt foolishly humiliated. I had just experienced something unclassifiable while she simply stretched her limbs like a cat. I collected my things and started up the lighthouse path. She saw that I was leaving and followed me at a distance. I longed to hate her.

Gruner was in quite a different mood when we got back to the lighthouse. As reserved as ever, he did not dare to tell me that he had changed his mind. The fellow was quite proud in certain aspects and would never admit to being suddenly convinced of an idea that he had once rejected. But his overtures at conversation could only mean one thing:

he wished to discuss the retrieval of the explosives. Still quite shaken, I ignored him for some time.

At last I insisted, "Five hundred beasts obliterated, perhaps six hundred. Or seven hundred. What say you?"

He still feigned doubt. Yet all the while, his hunter's lust blossomed.

"Have no fear," I joked without laughing or glancing at him. "If it goes badly and they eat us, I shall assume complete responsibility."

The mascot was squatted in a corner, scratching her crotch.

# 9

According to our speculations, dawn was the ideal moment to catch the monsters at rest. We headed toward the dinghy after yet another tumultuous night. Our minds were more alert than ever, despite our lack of sleep. Two trips were needed to haul the equipment over to the dinghy, which consisted of an air pump, a bronze diver's suit with its rubber lining, special lead-soled boots, rope, a portable pulley, weapons and munitions. We rowed out to the reef where the wreck lay. I craned my neck around from time to time. Under those circumstances, it seemed as if our destination was actually growing ever more distant rather than moving closer. It was barely one hundred yards away, but it felt like an eternity. Every pull of the tide was an ambush, every swell a quagmire. Rounded skulls appeared to emerge from the surrounding water. Floating branches, which bobbed aimlessly on the foam, resembled the beasts' grappling limbs. I trilled *va bene, va bene, va bene* on a half-hearted Italian whim. The melody calmed me.

"Shut your blasted mouth," Gruner said, rowing along with me like a galley slave.

A sepulchral stone grey weighed down the ocean's surface. We were hit by a spray of water from the side and my mouth filled with salt. Fear and urgency caused us to forget our own strength. The dinghy hit the reef with sudden force. Had it not been for the natural inclination of the rocks where our craft went aground, we most surely would have perished. The two of us disembarked on a rough and eroded boulder. It was a ridiculously small but labyrinth-like expanse, filled with concavities where half-frozen water pooled. It was treacherously slippery; we often had to catch hold with our arms to keep from falling.

Our plan was this: one could observe that the reef's gentle slope was riddled with useful notches. I would descend in the manner of an aquatic mountaineer. Gruner would work the air pump from his stone perch, hoisting up the crates as I lashed them. We were to share both labour and risks. I was to be the reckless soul paying a visit to Hades. He would have the no less arduous task of maintaining the flow of oxygen and retrieving the explosives. The pump had to maintain a regular and constant rhythm. Too little air and I would asphyxiate. Too much, and the excess pressure would burst my lungs. And Gruner had only one hand free to accomplish all this. He would be hoisting the dynamite up with the pulley at the same time. We placed the pump and pulley next to each other to ease the work. I was at the mercy of Gruner's coordination skills.

The ship had struck its prow against the reef, which pointed up at the sky at a thirty-degree angle from the starboard. The cargo was almost certainly to be found in the collapsed stern. Gruner attested that the vessel had ripped open like a tin can at the stern, leaving a great breach. We trusted that the opening was large enough for me to get through.

I donned the diver's suit and the lead-soled boots, taking a seat on the rocks alongside the dinghy. My torso was encased in a plate of bronze. The helmet came next. His body hunched over the headgear. But just as he was about to place it on my head I stopped him.

"Look," I said.

It was snowing. At first there were just specks. These were soon replaced by large round flakes. They fell and melted on contact with the water. It was snowing over the ocean; and this phenomenon, so simple as to be considered commonplace, produced a strange sensation within me. The snow imposed silence, like a conductor lifting his baton. The once choppy ocean had grown calm, as though tamed by some invisible force. This modest, almost banal beauty was to be perhaps my last vision of the world. I opened the palm of my hand. The flakes disintegrated the instant they landed on my gloves.

Gruner looked up at the sky, the helmet in his hands. He grimaced wryly.

"It is only snow," he said.

"Yes, it is only snow," I replied, "only snow. Come now, put the helmet on. We haven't got all day."

He screwed the metal dome in place, joining the air tube to its connection at the nape of my neck. I would carry two ropes with me. One would serve as a communication cord. The other was to hoist up the explosives.

"As you know," I reminded him, "if I pull on the communication cord once, then all goes well. Two tugs means that a crate is ready to be lifted. If you feel three tugs one after another, cut the tube with the axe and flee."

I adjusted the portholes on my helmet. There was one in front and on each side. I made sure the air tube was in working order and began my descent. Before I realised it, I was already under the waves. A shiver ran through me as I was engulfed by the frigid water. I made my way down the face of the reef. The vastness of the ocean was behind me. Dead rock lay only inches in front of my nose.

I lost my footing for an instant. It was no matter. I tugged once on the cord to reassure Gruner and let myself fall. The lead boots pulled me down slowly with calculated gravity until I landed on bent knee. A languid haze rose up to my waist. But it was just a thin sandy film obscuring the sun. The ocean floor was quite navigable, with a uniformly even surface. It was like walking across a field. But the liquid was palpably dense, and slowed every step.

Inside the helmet, I could hear nothing but my breathing, sniffles and an escaped moan of desperation. The two cords were in my left hand; my right grasped a knife. I observed my surroundings. There was nothing, not a single monster. Visibility was limited to twenty or thirty yards, perhaps less. The ship's hull was on my right. It resembled the cadaver of a whale. I sensed the immensity of the ocean before me. Unidentifiable particles floated aimlessly like specks of black snow. Serpent-shaped filaments of seaweed were suspended, practically motionless in the fluid. No door closed on this vast open space, the frontier of darkness was limitless.

The monsters might appear from out of nowhere any minute. Do not think about them, I told myself, just set your mind to the task. It was at once an eminently reasonable and wholly unrealistic strategy.

I made my way toward the stern. Gruner was right; the impact had sliced through the steel and twisted the metal sides into an artificial grotto. The vessel was slightly tipped to the starboard. The cargo had been displaced by the disaster and a good part of it was spilling out through the breach. This was a splendid piece of good fortune for it meant there was no need to enter the hold. Small metallic and rectangular containers were scattered about the edges of the wound. I ran my glove over the one nearest at hand. After a few swipes, one could make out the word DANGER!

All that remained was to lash a box with the cargo rope and tug on the communication cord once or twice. Gruner hoisted up the freight. The boxes were lifted over my head and out of sight. Gruner untied the dynamite and dropped the rope back down. The rope's tip was weighed down with a slug of lead. It fell somewhere nearby and I persevered with my labours.

I toiled with a miner's fervour until Gruner shook the cord uniting the two worlds. At first, I did not understand. Were we in danger? There was no trace of the monsters. No, no, that was not it. We had most likely collected too many boxes. But I was possessed by a prospector's fever for gold. One more, Gruner, just one more, I silently implored. Disregarding the jiggling cord, I fastened yet another crate. Gruner hefted it up, but this time the rope was returned with a knot around the lead weight telling me to stop. It required what little wits I had left to heed the warning.

As contradictory as it may seem, those were the worst moments of my foray. It is said that no soldier wants to be the last casualty of a war. This adage conceals an obscure and yet ever so human truth. To be killed after having plunged into the depths and achieved such an unmitigated success would have been an unthinkably cruel end. The diving suit took on a sudden and unbearable weight. Until then, I had not noticed that my neck was rubbed raw from the metal helmet. I advanced, dragging my feet, in the direction of the reef's face. The plodding desperation of my movements was reminiscent of a childhood nightmare. My breathing seemed propelled by some hidden dynamo. I longed to flee that spot, but it was impossible. The combined forces of two minds had not foreseen the most obvious flaw in our plan. The route down had been so precipitous that I could not retrace my steps. The rock face was riddled with cavities like the rotten tooth of a giant. I could not scale it, and Gruner would never be able to heft my bulk out of the water single-handedly. How long would it take for them to arrive? Terror joined forces with my imagination. That liquid expanse was the epitome of an unseen enemy. Gruner could not make sense of the air tube's bizarre twists and turns from his perch overhead. I scoured the rock in search of a navigable course, finally determining to begin my ascent at a point alongside the ship's hull. However, it demanded an almost herculean effort. The stone gave way underfoot in places. I slipped, falling five or ten yards in a single plunge.

I found myself once again on the ocean floor. There was a hollow in the rock on the right. I thought I saw something move within, some form. No, no, it is not them, I told myself. A prodigious effort of concentration followed. I had to find each foothold without looking or considering the monsters' jaws, so capable of carrying off an arm or a leg. I made sure that three out of four limbs were in place before continuing my ascent, just like a sailor climbing a rope ladder. The surface was already in sight. Gruner's silhouette encouraged me with his free hand through the water. I felt the damp release of my own urine within the diving suit.

Gruner leapt over and hoisted me out of the water by the armpits. He began to fumble with my helmet, but I swatted his hands away.

"Quickly, load the dynamite onto the dinghy!"

Once free of the suit, I too set to filling the little boat with boxes. The dinghy was so overloaded that it lay low in the water. Incredibly, in minutes we were on the island once again unscathed and triumphant. We left the dinghy quite close to the lighthouse on a small, sharp-stoned beach. Gruner immediately opened several of the containers, employing his axe handle as a lever. Each one contained seventy cartridges of dry and apparently active dynamite.

But a peculiar dementia smouldered within us. We set to glowering at one another. The snow fell harder than ever. Our hair was soon frosted white. We were of one mind as we looked first at the crates and then each other. I could not fathom an unspoken plot, I could not. There were cases of dynamite. One could wreak ruin with that quantity. But what if we possessed sixty? Why not eighty or one hundred? Our enemies were impervious to hate. They were a force of nature, akin to hurricanes or cyclones. Only now we were no longer powerless and could inflict a bloody revenge; now we were consumed by genuine cruelty. I suppose we had gone mad, so mad that we were conscious of our madness. I could hardly credit the words coming from my own mouth:

"We shall kill them all. Come, what do you say?"

"Yes, kill them all! Let's do it!" And so we returned to the dinghy as if that second suicidal excursion had been planned from the outset, as though someone else were to go in our place.

We rowed back to the reef and I put the diving suit back on. My movements underwater had improved with experience, they were swifter and better coordinated. There was no excuse. I was at the Portuguese ship's stern, wandering undefended through monster country. But the sight of those containers of dynamite brought forth visions of sunken pearls. We salvaged three, four, five. Ten, twenty. Finally, after having stirred up the ocean floor to uncover any hidden boxes, it seemed I had collected them all. I gave a tug to the communication cord: all was well.

There was a rent in the iron plate as if a Titan had bitten through the vessel's side. I entered with little difficulty. My only concern was whether or not the air tube would be able to follow my trajectory though the narrow passage. The route was ideal as there were no sharp edges to puncture my lifeline. There was the cargo, crammed with containers. I seized hold of one, secured it to the towrope and tipped it out of the vessel. Two pulls on the cord told Gruner to hoist up the load. I went about my work.

I had recovered about fifteen or twenty containers, perhaps more. Exhausted, I ceased moving so mechanically. Faint twilight bathed the hold in a dim light. The abundance of iron produced a sensation of claustrophobia. I was within the ship, within the diving suit and within my fears. It was fear and a ratlike heroism that had driven me down to those depths. It was the gloomiest place I had ever known. Walls of industrial metal, instruments half consumed by the salt water, obscured by rust. My lead boots made bizarre noises against the floor, echoing distortedly. The compartment had an open egg-shaped portal at one extreme. And that is where I spotted them, on the other side.

Only their eyes, peering at me impassively, could be distinguished in the gloom. How long had they been spying on me? I screamed within the narrow confines of the helmet. There was no escape. They were on home ground, manoeuvring the terrain with tremendous ease. I was beset by monsters from all directions, slicing through the water with my knife in a pathetic attempt to keep them at a distance.

But just when death seemed imminent, resurrection came. The helmet's glass amplified the scale of my surroundings. In truth, the monsters were barely a yard tall. Small thin bodies with a brilliant silvery grey band across their loins. It would be years before that strip would fade into the darker tone of their progenitors. The skull, as in human offspring, was disproportionately large. They were tadpoles in every way. The expression on their faces looked much like a dolphin's smile. They moved with prodigious speed like a flight of birds, eluding my bungled defence tactics. Their fingers pinched at my suit, especially the helmet, and then they shrank away. I imagine they associated the diving suit with some distant relative. Oh Lord, it dawned on me, they were just playing. Oh yes, playing. They had transformed that slag heap into a garden and I was an odd intruder. Their enthusiastic cries could best be described as chirping. My presence must have been an extraordinary novelty. I had expected butchers and found myself instead in the midst of an aquatic ballet.

I cannot tell for how long I was in their company. Contrary to all expectations, their presence lent that cemetery a beatific light. For the first time since disembarking, I was unafraid. I felt free of horror, as if it were dreadful ballast. The burden of persistent and systematic terror was such that I had scarcely been aware of it. I had lived in fear, both night and day, for months on end. I had wretchedly experienced every nuance of trepidation. Fear was my constant companion. Why, I asked myself, why has terror abandoned you precisely now, here in the bowels of hell? When I grasped one of the little fellows by the arm, the answer became clear. He too was not afraid. It was a monster, or at least a fledgling monster. The thing deserved to be twisted until his spine snapped. But he was unafraid. Just ticklish. He laughed. Yes, an underwater laugh. The tadpole laughed with his mouth, eyebrows and eyes while rubbing his little hands together. That laugh sounded like a hotel gong underwater. How much time had transpired since I myself had laughed? I let him go. Rather than run away, he flew about me like an erratic butterfly, laughing all the while. His little hand touched the helmet's glass with foetuslike fingers. He touched the glass and the memory of those little grey fingers haunted me for days.

I left the wreck. The creatures kept me company throughout my ascent. They wound round my body, poking me with sweet impertinence, like playful kittens nipping away. Their numbers lessened the closer I got to the dinghy. Gruner was in a sulk when I got to the surface.

"I began to think you had taken up residence! *Mein Gott*, what the devil was going on down there?"

My legs gave way. He removed the helmet and saw the delirious face of an envoy who, in his exhaustion, no longer recalls his message.

"Toads?" he asked nervously.

"No, baby dolphins!"

Gruner stepped back a pace. He observed me as though attempting to gauge my mental health.

"You came up too quickly," he proclaimed. "The hallucinations will soon pass."

Suddenly Gruner appeared to have been infected by the very dementia he had diagnosed me with. Muffling a scream, he seized the rifle, which hung from his shoulder. A head emerged from the water close by.

From atop a rock, I held up my arm. "Do not shoot! For the love of God, Gruner, hold your fire!"

Gruner's eyes roved back and forth between me and the motionless monster.

"Do not shoot," I insisted, "it is no more than a baby."

Gruner was not quick enough. By the time the gun was poised, the ocean was once again an empty surface.

# 10

The landscape had undergone a transformation while we were out on the water. The trees were covered in snow, their branches bowed under a burden of white. The path through the woods had been obliterated, wiped out. Our feet were the first to sully that intact carpet. The habitually grim atmosphere of that inhospitable land had been replaced by an ivory coating, lending our residence a painful sweetness. The snow had buried all evidence of battle, covering the rocks and the lighthouse's peak. The piles of detritus, which had accumulated some fifty-five yards from the tower, had disappeared from view beneath a blanket of sugar. Even the reefs nearby were swathed in a white heap, lapped by the waves. The sight was intoxicating. I was still overcome by the monsters' young, and the snow rekindled those sensations of painful tenderness. We unpacked the explosives. Although my body carried out the task, my mind was elsewhere.

Gruner knew no rest. His bellicose spirit was well suited to the work. We counted and ordered the cartridges. There was enough dynamite to demolish half of London.

Our own stores contained hundreds of feet of waterproof wick and three detonators with T-shaped plungers. They formed part of the supplies required for any military building project. The ordinances stipulated that they be used to destroy the lighthouse in case of war. The wicks and detonators, either out of forgetfulness or incompetence, had been left behind in a corner. Or perhaps the island had been evacuated more suddenly than Gruner claimed. Who knows?

That was where Gruner's labours ended and my imagination took over. We could always make use of the cartridges as individual hand grenades. But I aspired to greater things. The detonators and wicks gave us an added advantage. My idea was to devise three devastating blasts.

The first explosions would be aligned directly in front of the rock foundation. That was our last line of defence, and for safety's sake, it was also the weakest charge. Not being experts, we were unable to gauge the dynamite's power with any certainty. The entire lighthouse could be blown to bits if we were not careful.

The second line of charges would be situated approximately twenty yards away, at the edge of the woods. A long wick, buried in the snow, linked the chain of cartridges. That was to be the site of the most potent explosion. It was a logical choice as we anticipated that most of the monsters would congregate there, between the rocks and the forest. Our plan was to scour the terrain from coast to coast, digging little hollows in which to hide the munitions.

The third line of combat was to be even farther away, within the forest itself, camouflaged by the trees. It served a vital function. The charges could be activated whenever we wished. They might be set off first, sending the monsters in a mass retreat to the second string of explosives. Or they could be detonated afterwards, so as to pick off the few remaining survivors.

We toiled all day, binding together bundles of ten cartridges, joining them to a single wick and burying them. The entire operation was repeated a bit farther on. The wick was uncoiled once we reached the end of a row, yard by yard, until it reached the lighthouse. The cord was nailed along the stone wall and up to the balcony, where we had placed the detonators. The mascot also helped, without knowing why.

The darkness gathered about us quickly. But the monsters did not. It was unbelievable. After so many nights of warding off death's door, they suddenly chose not to appear. As the hours passed, impatience turned to exasperation.

"Where are they, where the devil are they?" I called into the void.

Gruner kept a more composed vigil. He contented himself by tracing the beacon's path with the tip of his rifle. The light revealed only indolent flakes of snow as it pierced the darkness. There was no trace of a footprint, aside from those our boots had left behind, to mar the snowy landscape. My hands were sweating. I was forever putting on and taking off my gloves or brushing the snow out of my beard. Had they been kept away by the storm?

The next evening brought little change. We spotted a few, or we heard them I should say. They croaked in an amphibious chorus for no apparent reason. The first rays of sun unveiled two, three, four or five beasts. No, there must have been more. They wandered erratically along the edges of the forest without venturing near. It was not worth wasting a bullet on them, let alone the dynamite. The following nights were the same. They were there and yet they were not.

The most extravagant ideas flitted through my head, like flies buzzing about a pigsty, as the situation stagnated. I took to investigating the three lines of explosives and the interconnected bundles buried in the snow. Resembling an explorer in every way, I kneeled down to inspect the monsters' footprints, so as to discover what predatory logic lay behind their actions. Had they somehow sniffed out the dynamite? Did that gregarious horde suspect a new and thus more fearful danger than the already familiar firearms? Sometimes I surprised myself as vapour escaped from my mouth, searching for meaning in the veritable labyrinth of monstrous footprints. What if they were actually as bright as pennies? As much as possible, we had threaded the wick through scrap sections of tube and pipe before burying it. None of this had been touched.

During this lull, I bedded the mascot yet again. I brought her with me with the habitual excuse of collecting scrap metal. For lack of any other occupation, I spent my days reinforcing cartridges with layers of scrap metal, nails, stones or any other small sharp object on hand. The weather official's cottage suited my needs perfectly. We literally ransacked the space in search of makeshift munitions. Before or after the sacks were loaded, I splayed the beast across the floor and possessed her.

Philosophy and love fight their battles in intangible realms. But war and lust are purely matters of the flesh. Fornicating with the mascot was a kind of consensual rape. My arms were unable to encompass the totality of her body, the surface of such skin. I treated her as though I were putting down a useless farm animal. After having copulated with her, I was filled with a feeling of genuine hate toward that messenger of evil.

Such immeasurable pleasure had lost its novelty. But it was in no way diminished. I lay with her two, three, perhaps four times. I felt a singular sort of sadness afterwards, a childlike helplessness. I was a lover without a lover, a lost man wandering in circles through the desert. The cottage's lamentable state increased my malaise. The place brought to mind a miniature Rome, ravaged by over thousands of years of barbarian invasion. The mascot at my side, I lay on a pile of dirty, clammy blankets, stiff as cardboard. Meanwhile, the ruinous cottage scrutinised me like an ant under a microscope. Stalactites of ice grew from the leaks in the roof. Due to the damp, the wooden planks of the walls had warped like sunflowers bending toward the light. Time slackened its pace in that hovel; one saw life from the minute perspective of a fly. Those days I felt poised within those walls halfway between life and death. I was left with but two instincts: love and murder. Both were denied to me. The monsters did not come, and she was a monster.

Gruner would proclaim from time to time, "They shall come today," with the air of a peasant predicting the weather. But he was always mistaken. They had simply vanished. The monsters treated us with disdain rather than wariness. When we did spot one or two, it was pure coincidence. Small flocks could be heard moving about beyond the beacon's limited scope. They yowled under an evening snowfall or surveyed us in silence, but they never attacked the lighthouse. It seemed as if the beasts traversed the island's murky paths with a precise destination in mind, choosing the most direct route through the forest. That was all. One day, in an attempt to drive those howlers out of the thicket, we set off different-coloured flares. It was useless.

I should never have imagined that I would one day long to be attacked by a horde of monsters. In fact, their continued absence had driven me to the brink of exasperation. One day I found Gruner sitting in a chair outside. I brought out another. My seat happened to be a bit wobbly. I lost my balance and fell quite ridiculously. We had very little furniture and it could have been mended easily. Instead, I smashed it against the lighthouse wall. I broke its legs and backrest and then jumped up and down on the remaining shards until nothing was left to tell that it had once been a chair. Gruner observed me all the while, taking swigs from a bottle of rum. He kept his mouth shut.

Another day, I came very close to murdering the mascot. I do not recall the details, and truthfully, it makes no difference. I believe she was carrying firewood. She had three trunks in her arms and one fell. When she went to lift it off the ground she clumsily dropped the second. The beast bent down to pick up the second and dropped the third. This inane pantomime was repeated again and again. I drew near. "Pick up the trunks," I said. She tried and failed. I slapped the nape of her neck with the back of my hand. "Collect the logs!" She was terrified by my insistence. "Gather those logs!" She shook with fear. I seized her by the neck. "Gather up those logs!" The mascot shrieked for help, and this infuriated me. Yes, I would most surely have killed her if Gruner had not appeared.

"Friend, she is just a toad."

It must be understood that, more than a display of piety, his words were a declaration of ownership. My mistreatment of the mascot affected him to the extent that it challenged his sovereignty over her, and nothing more.

"Yes, a toad. And only one. That is the problem," I said, and strode away.

I was loath to admit the obscure causes of my frustration. Above all, there was one, quite obvious matter. I had staked my life on the deep-sea adventure to the Portuguese wreck. And by some incomprehensible coincidence, my gamble coincided with the enemy's utter apathy. It was aggravating. I had felt like a proper bourgeois who expects recompense for his efforts after such an excursion. What was more, I believed, or wished to believe, that a massacre would eradicate every hounding danger and extinguish our inferno once and for all. On the other hand, the monsters themselves filled me with a dread I could scarcely put into words. That little hand pressing against the glass of my diving helmet. The mascot's lust. In the daytime, my wayward mind entertained the hallucinations of an opium addict. Gruner was before me, muttering a few monosyllables, and I replied, more or less. But I did not pay close attention. The space between us became populated with hazy visions.

I saw that tiny hand underwater. Those minute fingers rubbed the glass with such innocence and assurance. I saw the mascot, and the memory of her writhing body enthralled me as though the air were the screen of a magic lantern. Every angle of that concupiscence was at once foreign and yet ever so undemanding.

As contradictory as it may seem, the more pleasure the mascot gave me, the more I loathed her. She seemed to be the embodiment of every other beast. The fact that the others should inspire such horror and the mascot such pleasure may perhaps explain the nervous fits I suffered. Think, think, think, I said to myself, striking my forehead with a closed fist.

"Gruner," I said one day, "we must be daring. Tempt them somehow. We ought to leave the door open."

Before he could protest, I hastened to add, "It is not as dangerous as it seems. All things considered, they can only climb the spiral staircase one by one. A marksman at the trapdoor might easily shoot them down. And it should never come to that. The idea is to get the beasts flocking about the lighthouse. Once they are all together, send them sky high."

Gruner had defended the lighthouse, alone or accompanied, for an eternity, and not once had the monsters managed to set foot in his sanctum. Now I was proposing to leave that door open, the door of his lighthouse.

"One thousand monsters dead, Gruner," I said, in hopes that a number might awaken the fellow's limited imagination.

"Who will activate the detonators?"

The question exposed Gruner's puerile side. There are two sorts of combatants: strategists and those who have never gone beyond a childish need to break things. I saw myself as the former and Gruner the latter.

"As you wish," I placated him. "If you like, I shall guard the trapdoor while you send them to hell."

And so it was settled. I opened the door at dusk. A lit lantern was placed on every twentieth step. That way, in case they did get in, we would be able to shoot them down with ease. I would merely point the Remington out of the open trapdoor. Not even the worst shot misses his mark at point-blank range. Gruner was on the balcony and I covered his back, the staircase being under control.

"Well, do you see them?" I demanded.

"No."

I waited a bit.

"And now? And now, Gruner?"

"No, nothing. Absolutely nothing."

I wanted to see for myself and, driven by impatience, went over to the balcony.

"Return to your post!" yelled Gruner. "Go back, I say! Do you want us killed?"

There was sense in what he said. They were more than capable of evading the beam's path and taking us by surprise. Still, I did not see anything either, except the tenuous light from the lanterns strewn up the twisting steps. The flames trembled and glowed in the draughty air.

"Two," Gruner stated.

"Where, where?" I cried out from my post.

"To the west. They are coming this way. Four or five. I cannot make an exact count."

"Hold your fire. Let them get close. Above all, they must see the open door."

That telegraphic interchange grated on my nerves. Gruner shifted from side to side on the tiny balcony, surveying the darkness. I aimed the Remington down into the void below while keeping my eyes trained on Gruner. I asked him again and again if there was any change outside, neglecting my duty. It was nearly a fatal error. The sound of breaking glass drew my attention. The first few lanterns had gone out.

"Gruner, they are already here!" I warned.

One could hear them howling below. I barely distinguished the outlines of a claw as it snatched at the third lantern. Whole sections of the staircase were snuffed out with that swipe. The ground floor was a black well, a pit from which rose a chorus of croaking. Suddenly a lone monster rushed up the stairs on all fours. They no longer bothered to extinguish the lights; one could discern his slithering form perfectly. The remaining kerosene lamps illuminated the monster's belly eerily from below, making him look even more diabolical. The beast was heading straight for me, practically hurling himself against the rifle. Should I fire? If I did so, his companions outside might turn back. We wanted a massacre. I could hear Gruner calling my name, but did not have time to explain; the monster advanced as swiftly as a lizard. Just when there were only ten, nine, eight steps between us, the monster stopped short. The last kerosene lamp was quite close to his face. We stared at each other, I from the opening in the floor and he eight steps away from the cannon. The kerosene lamp was all that separated us. Those close quarters were infused with a vast rancour as the monster and I held each other's gaze. He seemed to be taken straight from a vision of Saint Anthony. We took stock of each other's strength and capabilities. The monster spread his arms wide and leaned against the step above. That stance revealed a vital detail: a chunk of membrane and half of a finger were missing from one hand. It was him. Our circumstances had changed quite a bit since our first encounter. I was no longer a helpless prisoner. We abhorred each other as only two equals do. My instinct told me to annihilate him right then and there. Logic argued that I should let him live to tell the others about the open door. I struck a compromise between reason and emotion. The thing would be riddled with bullets if he took one more step.

"Move, you wild son of Babylon," I whispered while taking aim, "just one more step."

The monster growled. But before any decision could be made, Gruner's gun rang out. The man was shooting at the others. My monster opened his mouth, flicking his tongue back and forth. The gesture managed to express at once impotence and disdain. He retraced his steps. The monster retreated slowly, without turning around. He left each step behind as grudgingly as an emperor cedes territory. Once the beast was safely away, I asked Gruner for an explanation.

"And the dynamite? May I ask why the devil the explosives were not activated?"

Despite the vehemence of my tone, he remained calm. He argued his case in a coldly calculating manner: "They were too numerous to be allowed inside and not enough to employ the dynamite."

With those words, Gruner summed the matter up. The fellow had acted for the best. All we had longed for since scavenging the wreck, all we had awaited night after night, was to arrive the very next day.

It snowed throughout the day with a Nordic persistence. A knee-deep coating lay on the ground. The sun had already begun to set by early afternoon, dragging the dusk behind as if refusing to bear witness. The mascot had sung without pause or rest ever since, her eyes closed. It was the most destructive melody I had ever heard. I recall how Gruner and I ate together off steel dishes in absolute silence. We would occasionally exchange glances, or look at her. It disturbed us more than ever. But we had not the will to still her eerie chant. These and other omens foretold the coming developments.

We smoked after dinner. Gruner rubbed his beard and stared at the floor. We were like two strangers chatting in a train station.

"Gruner," I asked out of curiosity, "have you ever been in a war?"

"Who, me?" Gruner asked impassively. "No, but I did work as a forest warden for a time. I assisted hunters, wealthy Italians mostly. We shot wild boars and bears. Have you ever been in the military?"

"One can undergo all the dangers of war without ever having held a gun," I said.

"When a bear gets shot, it falls just like a man. Watch."

Gruner contorted his body, twisting his neck and shoulders. For a moment, I was sure he would fall to the floor for added realism.

Instead he said, wide-eyed, "A flesh wound on a bear looks no different than one on our arms or legs." After a long pause he went on. "One doesn't realise it, but it is far worse to kill a wild boar than a bear. Far worse. It is not so much the way they twitch as how they wail. Imagine the sound of a trumpet packed with stones. A very big trumpet."

"Screams have been filling my dreams of late," I said. "Just cries, no images. I don't know who is screaming."

"Sometimes it takes as much as five bullets to finish off a wild boar," Gruner continued. "They do not want to die. And they won't shut up until they are dead."

It was always the same with us. We would appear to be conversing on the surface, but it was actually nothing more than an interchange of monologues. There was a lapse of dead silence. I gazed up at the sky without moving from my seat. The snowstorm had died down into gentle flurries. We would have a full moon. Falling stars appeared before it rose, intruders in the violet dusk. They flared as briefly as a match flame, and were far too fleeting to wish upon.

Gruner said with a childish curiosity, "How is it you were in a war without ever having fired a gun?"

I pointed to our arsenal with one finger. "Remember to twist the plunger three times before activating the detonators. If they don't gather enough energy, they won't ignite. Understood?"

I scattered the remaining kerosene lamps along the stairs. I assumed my position at the trapdoor, lying on the floor with the rifle in hand. From time to time I would pester Gruner for information.

"No toads, no toads," he said. Half an hour went by. A gust of snow blew in through the open door below. It was only snow, nothing more.

"Are they here yet, Gruner? Do you see them coming?"

He gave no reply. I had learned my lesson the night before and did not dare turn around. I wanted to keep my eyes on the storeroom and the open door.

"Gruner?"

I glanced over at him quickly. He was on the balcony, kneeling behind the barricade of sacks. Something out in the gloom had paralysed Gruner; he resembled a pillar of salt.

I called his name to break the trance which possessed him. "Gruner, are they coming?"

He did not move a single muscle. I left the trapdoor, against my better judgment, and took hold of his elbow. "Are you chilled? Shall I take up your post?"

"*Mein Gott, mein Gott . . .*"

My ears were greeted by a cacophony of voices, much like the sound of blocked pipes. I peered over the balcony.

Their numbers exceeded the most perverse fantasy. The full moon, magnified by the southern latitude, cast a theatrical light over the island. The horde overtook the landscape, amassing in the forest, shaking the trees and dislodging clumps of snow. There were so many that they skittered up and down the branches, one on top of the other. The crowd was so dense that many had no choice but to watch from the reefs along the coast, like reptiles in the sun. Exasperated and frenetic, they could barely move their arms for lack of space. The scene resembled a fisherman's bucket, swarming with live bait. The stronger ones trampled the weak, even injuring them if need be, as they scampered over their bald skulls. A doughy mass of grey and green flesh halted before the rock foundation, pulling back indecisively, as though awaiting the orders of some unknown leader.

"Gruner, activate the detonators!"

But he was deaf to my entreaties. His lower lip drooped as though a heavy earring were weighing it down. He gripped the rifle with both hands without aiming at anything in particular.

"Gruner, Gruner, Gruner!" I shook him by the shoulders.

He lowered the Remington even more. He looked at me without recognition and whispered, "Who are you? Where are we? Where are we? Where?"

I had no time to help the man. I merely told him to stand, pulling him to his feet by the scruff of the neck.

Gruner gazed abstractedly at his chest and hands, oblivious of the encroaching catastrophe. In a way I envied him.

I decided to activate the charges clustered around the foundation first. The plunger went all the way down. Gruner, still in a trance, and I stared at each other like a pair of fools for a second. It did not go off. But all at once a thunderous explosion threw us to the floor. The railings twisted as if they were wire. The entire building teetered. I had the impression of being within the Leaning Tower of Pisa. My eyes, once open, were met with the sight of Gruner coated from head to foot in dust and ash. An opaque cloud lurked within the lighthouse. Particles of glimmering soot flitted about. One could dimly distinguish the mascot's outline, shrieking in terror.

I propped my elbows over the barricade. Dozens, or rather hundreds, of monsters had been exterminated. The cadavers were scattered about, the dying jumbled in with the dead.

"Gruner, I need your help!"

The survivors ignored the dead. Screeching all the while, they rushed at the open door. Gruner, either somewhat recovered or completely mad, opened fire on the multitude. I followed suit, working the lock with each shot. The shells flew at machine-gun speed. It was impossible to miss. They perished as fanatics, their falling bodies blocking the advance of those behind.

"Continue firing," I bellowed, throwing the rifle aside. "Don't let them near the door!"

I had meant to activate the second round of explosives, but was distracted by the confusion of battle. Instead of setting off the second row of dynamite, I blew up the third one, which lay farthest away. Half of the forest was sent heavenward.

A black and scarlet mushroom rose twenty-five or thirty yards high. The trees burned like matchsticks despite the blanket of snow. Many flew into the air, twisting over the axis of their roots and then tumbling down. The stakes were studded with body parts. The carnage bombarded us like cannonballs. A cranium smashed against the balcony's shutters just as we were met with the full force of the blast. The explosion swept away the barricade like a tropical hurricane and I went along with it. Suddenly I was back in the lighthouse, dragging myself by the elbows through an asphyxiating black cloud of smoke. The floor was littered with sand and leaping sparks. Somewhere outside, bundles of dynamite exploded seconds apart, one after another. My breath was tainted with sulphur. I coughed and spat, and saw the mascot, defenceless in a corner. We stared at each other in puzzlement for a moment. She did not understand what was going on at first and neither did I. What was happening? The sheer strength of the explosion exceeded our wildest expectations. Gruner had been unable to resist the temptation of adding extra cartridges on the sly. We had agreed to set aside some of the dynamite just in case. But he had undoubtedly added every charge we possessed to the buried wicks. If the first and third lines of dynamite had come very near to killing us, what would happen when we set off the second, most powerful charge?

"Gruner!"

He was on the balcony, dirty and unharmed. The haze of a London-like fog lent him a ghostly air. A good part of his hair had been singed and was still smouldering. He waved the Remington about with one hand as if it were a pistol. His other fist was raised against the enemy. Incredibly, a monster managed to slither up in between the stakes to the ravaged railing. Gruner broke the beast's skull with his rifle butt, opening it like a melon in a brutal surfeit of blows. Then he shifted his attention over to the last detonator.

"Gruner, don't do it, don't do it, whatever you do, don't!" I screamed, down on my knees and grasping him about the waist. "We shall be blown to bits!"

He looked at me for a moment with the indulgence of a feudal lord and said, "Move aside!"

He shoved me down against the fallen barricade.

Below, the monsters roasted in a burning trap. They searched for the ocean and found only curtains of fire. Many of the living fled, enveloped in flames. The blaze had consumed over half of the island. The terrified monsters, scorched red against the inky night, created the eerie effect of a Chinese shadow puppet theatre. Demented wails rose up to the balcony. Gruner bore down on the plunger.

It seemed the island would be torn asunder like a cannoned ship. An incandescent dome rose from north to south. Our lighthouse took on a ridiculous insignificance, the fragility of a lily in a rainstorm. A tide of debris and mud had covered everything in sight. Suddenly the monsters' howls, Gruner's, even mine became as one. I had gone deaf, capable only of watching Gruner's lips move in the midst of that artificial silence. I saw mutilated bodies soar to astonishing heights. The explosion appeared to be a living thing, a genie conjured up by Gruner. Oblivious to the surrounding havoc, Gruner clapped, danced and swore as though he were under the influence of a witch's potion. One last avalanche rushed through the balcony door and a torrent of detritus bathed us in frigid magma. All together, it was a scene out of Revelations.

The following events are of little importance. Gruner and I sat far apart. We shunned each other, trapped in our own ignominy. If that was victory, nobody cared to mention, let alone celebrate, such butchery. Two hours later I began to hear the distant whistle of a locomotive. My ears began to slowly open again to the world of sounds. By daybreak, they were almost completely recovered.

We readied ourselves for a most macabre task. Scarves

and handkerchiefs swathed our noses. We ventured out at first light. A dim glow of candlelight illuminated the landscape. It was horrible. Flames had stained the lighthouse black. Encrusted shrapnel gave it the look of a face horribly rutted by pox. The gunnysacks on the balcony, riddled with holes, leaked their contents like hourglasses.

A gigantic crater marked the sight of the last explosion. As for the monsters, they were strewn about as though cut down by an avenging angel. The number of casualties was incalculable. They were on all sides. Many were floating on the water's surface. Mutilated, blackened, their limbs were mummified by fire. Doubled over like rag dolls, their claws rigid and their mouths open. I shall never forget the stench of burnt flesh, a smell horribly similar to boiled vinegar. Some bodies were so consumed that their charred ribs emerged like curved black bars. Others were still moving. Putting them out of their misery was, above all, an act of compassion. We walked among the dead and, at the merest movement, stabbed the creatures in the neck. Gruner wielded his harpoon, and I a long knife. But the spectacle brought out Gruner's most sadistic nature.

One of them had been left with half a leg on one side; the other limb had been blown clean off. The monster was nothing more than a carcass, trailing white smoke behind as it dragged itself along by the elbows. Instead of killing the creature, Gruner stepped in front of it. The monster saw a pair of boots impeding its progress and changed direction in fits and starts. Gruner blockaded the beast's path to the coast at every turn. But the monster, stubborn as an ox, did not give in, searching for the ocean with snail-like movements.

"Sacrifice it, for God's sake!" I yelled, ripping the handkerchief from my mouth. He continued to amuse himself for a while longer. Then he drove the harpoon through the creature's neck.

We spent an untold length of time dumping bodies into the ocean. We had not even come close to completing the task when I spotted the mascot on the balcony. She was sitting cross-legged and held the bars as if in a cage.

"My God," I exclaimed, "look at her!"

"Who is wailing now?" asked Gruner.

"My God, she is crying."

# 11

Disaster struck with the cruelty of surprise. Not forty-eight hours had passed since the infamous butchery. Two days, two fleeting days of peace. I found myself wandering somewhere in the forest, armed with a pencil and notebook in an attempt to reconstruct the calendar. I had long since lost track of the exact date. Gruner never bothered with such matters, and I had kept records only sporadically. During the most perilous spells, I neglected to cross off the days simply because I had little hope of seeing the morrow. Pages of the calendar had been marked twice over. There was an entire month of miscalculation. One could trace the confusion of shaky lines, which shifted between black and red. The black ink crossed out each day. But the red tint did not pay the black any attention. It started all over again on the same month; doodles filled each square to baroque excess. Every date took on a fanciful form. The first of February was a monster lying in wait, the second was a crouching beast about to pounce, the eighth was a heap of bodies climbing up the lighthouse's side, the eleventh was a tower of amphibians.

I no longer recalled having engendered such madness and was unable to recognise it as my own. Naturally, I was at first filled with delight by the discovery. If time had been artificially held back, it could only mean my ship would arrive sooner than expected. But a closer inspection of my miscalculations, the days twice crossed out, showed I had nothing to celebrate. According to the calendar, my ship should have come two weeks ago.

What had gone wrong? Had yet another world war brought all naval traffic to a standstill until the hostilities were over? Perhaps. Humanity has a tendency to blame our sufferings on the great hecatombs in order to bestow more importance on our individual lives. But truth is almost always written in lowercase letters. I was the last grain of sand on this infinite beach called Europe; a solitary soldier in the trenches; a subject without a king. Most likely some inept bureaucrat had banished the meteorological expedition to the wrong filing cabinet. The chain of command had broken at some point; that was all. One could be quite certain that my plight would never be discussed at a meeting of the board of directors.

I remember riffling through the calendar pages nervously, trying in vain to disprove my own fatal calculations. I recall the black nail of my index finger counting the paper squares like some dismal accountant. It was no use. Desperation began to take hold, a castle crumbling in my gut. That calendar scheduled my doom, condemned me to a life sentence. I longed for death. And yet, the best way to forget bad news is to be told something worse. Could such a thing exist? Yes.

I simply could not credit Gruner's warning voice calling out *"Zum Leuchtturm!"* from the balcony. Something very fragile broke within my soul on hearing those bullets rip through the cold air. I was not aware of it at first. I dropped pencil and paper and ran for dear life.

They did not wait for the cover of darkness. Slithering forms emerged at the first sign of dusk, circling the scorched and shrapnel-pitted lighthouse. "Friend, friend," Gruner cautioned as his rifle spat in all directions. The explosions had reduced the stone steps to rubble. I clambered my way up to the door. Gruner covered my back. He took aim at the monsters as they drew perilously close. They appeared and disappeared with each shot. My fear turned to rage just as I was about to reach safety. Why had they returned? We had slaughtered hundreds. And here they were once more. Instead of seeking refuge, I began to stone the beast closest by. I hurled rocks at his face; one, two, three. I can still hear myself cursing. The monster threw its arms over its head and stepped back. And then a most extraordinary thing occurred; the beast threw a stone at me! It was at once horrid and grotesquely ridiculous. Gruner exterminated it with one well-placed shot.

"Friend, come inside. What are you waiting for?"

I took up my position on the balcony, firing one or two shots. The monsters were few in number, but they were there.

I lowered my weapon. Their very presence proved the futility of it all. No matter what, they would always come back, and in greater numbers. A bullet or an explosion was as much a natural catastrophe as a rainstorm was to an ant. Our efforts might lower their numbers, but never their perseverance. I raised the white flag of surrender.

"Where the devil are you going now?" Gruner challenged.

Lacking the will to reply, I sat in a chair, my head in my hands and a rifle across my knees. I began to sob like a child. The mascot was before me. Oddly enough, she too was seated in a chair, leaning indolently against the table. But, as usual, she contemplated Gruner on the balcony, the gunfire, my tears and the attacks on the lighthouse with the indifference of a museumgoer gazing at a painted battle scene.

My courage, forbearance and wits had been stretched to untold limits. I had fought the monsters with weapons and without, on land and sea, under cover and out in the open. And every night, if it suited their fancy, they returned in ever greater numbers. The beasts seemed impervious to destruction. Gruner kept up the assault. But that battle no longer belonged to me. "Oh dear God," I sputtered, and rubbed my tear-stained cheeks, what more could a reasonable man do in my position? What should the most resolute, the wisest man have done that I had not yet tried?

My gaze shifted back and forth between my moist palms and the mascot. She had been crying not two days before. Now it was I who wept. Those tears had undone something more than my body. A rampant tide of memories swept over me. One thinks most freely after weeping.

The mascot and I held each other's gaze the whole night through. Gruner fought while we stared across the table at each other until I could no longer tell who I was looking at nor who was looking at me.

Afterwards, Gruner disdained me as if I were a deserter. In the morning, he left to go for a walk, or something of that sort. I went into his quarters immediately afterwards. The mascot slept huddled up in a corner of the bed, naked save for a pair of socks. I seized her by the scruff of the neck and sat her down at the table.

Gruner was met with a delirious man at midday.

"Gruner," I said, brimming with enthusiasm, "guess what I have done today?"

"Waste time. I had to buttress up the door all by myself."

"Come with me."

I led the mascot along by the elbow and Gruner

followed a step behind. I forced her to sit down once we were outside the lighthouse. Unfazed, he remained standing next to me.

"Observe."

I piled one, two, three, four blocks of firewood under my arm. The fourth however, I purposely let fall. I was clowning about, of course. As I collected a trunk, another would slip from the bundle. I repeated the sequence again and again. As usual, Gruner watched me with his puzzled look, but did not interrupt. Oh, come on, come on, I thought. I had carried out the experiment that morning, while Gruner was away. But I failed to get any results now. As Gruner glared at me, I kept my eyes on the mascot and she watched the logs.

At last, she laughed. The truth is, it required a bit of imagination to recognise it as a laugh as such. But that is exactly what it was. The sound resonated up from the mascot's chest. Strident tones could be heard through her mouth, clamped shut. The inner workings of some unseen muscle reached our ears. Then her lips parted. There could be no doubt, it was laughter.

"You see?" I said with triumphal satisfaction. "You see? What do you think now?"

"I think that my good fellow friend is incapable of carrying four logs at the same time."

"Gruner, she is laughing!" I paused, waiting for a

reaction that never presented itself. I added, "She cries, she laughs. What is your conclusion?"

"Conclusion?" he bellowed. "I shall tell you what my conclusion is! They breed like rabbits. The beasts will charge to battle once again, and not as they have the last few nights, but in the thousands. It shall be our last evening on earth. And in the meantime, you entertain yourself by fiddling with four sticks like a fairground clown."

But all I could think of was her. What was she doing at the lighthouse, with such a brute as her sole companion? I knew very little about her. Gruner once told me how he found her splayed out on the sand, like one of the jellyfish that washed up on our beaches.

"She has never attempted escape or tried to leave the island?" I enquired. Gruner paid me no mind. I persisted, "You often beat her. She ought to abhor your presence. But she does not run away. It is not as though there has been any want of opportunity."

"Sir, you have had odd ideas of late."

"Yes, and I cannot help entertaining a reckless idea," I announced. "What if they are something more than just monstrous amphibians?"

"Something more than just monstrous amphibians . . ." he repeated unhearing while counting our ever-dwindling supply of ammunition.

"Why not? Perhaps there is something besides instinct

lurking beneath those bald skulls. If that is the case," I continued, "it might be possible to negotiate."

"And I think you ought to rein in your imagination," he interjected, loading his shotgun with exaggerated gusto.

Nothing was to be gained from arguing, and I preferred to save myself for other battles.

Undoubtedly, the attacks were few and far between. The mascot had ceased her song, which gave us a small measure of security. But we could not deceive ourselves. Constant combat had lent us an imperceptible but palpable awareness. The sea was rough, the waves stained eggplant. The air was so saturated with damp one could envisage a school of whales sporting about the sky. Small signs which normally should have been meaningless took on an irrational importance. Without our being able to explain quite why, it seemed that doomsday was upon us. Forces were gathering beneath the waves, and this time our diminished arsenal would be unable to stop them.

Every omen foretold our death. Perhaps that was why I took up with the mascot again, because nothing mattered. Not many precautions were needed to conceal ourselves from Gruner. Death was about to disembark on the island, our death, and that was enough for Gruner to take shelter in his interior world. He escaped from reality by repairing a door or counting our few remaining cartridges. Gruner could tell each one apart just as a farmer knows his cows; he even named them. He set the prettiest bullets aside – I know not what criteria he used to differentiate them – and wrapped them in a silk handkerchief. Then Gruner would untie the knot and count them all over again. He gently fingered each slug with eyes half shut as if he were never quite sure of the exact number. Gruner well knew how much this meticulousness annoyed me. Therefore it was natural, if only to avoid unwanted tensions, for me to leave the lighthouse. I spent those long interludes having my way with the mascot. Our trysts usually took place in the forest. I seldom ventured to the weather official's house, for fear of Gruner's unexpected appearance.

As a result, my interactions with Gruner became quite sporadic during those days of lingering agony. Worse yet, the mood within the lighthouse had grown obscurely tainted. It was not so much what we said as what we had ceased to say. We had not yet determined to commit suicide and I needed something to entertain my thoughts. I recalled *The Golden Bough*.

"Do you know where that book by Frazer has gone? I have been looking around these last few days and haven't been able to find it."

"Book? What book? I do not read books. What do you think I am, a monk?"

I did not believe a word he said. Why was he lying? Did he abhor me so much as to deny me the consolations of reading? In his own way, Gruner could be quite diplomatic.

The fellow kicked me from the chair where he was seated. "You want books, some sort of a distraction? You are a young fellow. Perhaps we should capture a lady toad for your amusement." Then he sneered at me in a profoundly disagreeable and ironic manner. Did he suspect anything? No. He was just being provocative. Gruner wanted me to leave the room so he could fornicate with the mascot at his ease. I had no wish to smooth his way.

"The last thing one may say about this island," I replied, "is that it lacks distractions. The solution to our troubles may very well be right in front of our noses."

He attempted to disguise his sarcasm. "Oh really?" He crossed his arms in sudden interest. "Tell me then. Is your pupil making any progress? Exactly what skills is she being taught? French cuisine? Chinese calligraphy? Or are you perfecting the four-log juggling act?"

He was fooling himself. The question was not so much what she could learn from us as what we might learn from her. The most devastating thing about it all was how, in fact, nothing had changed. We were like landscape painters trying to depict a storm with their backs to the horizon. We simply needed to turn around, nothing more.

Insignificant details were deciding factors: she smiled,

was clearly left-handed, could not tolerate being pursued and squatted to urinate. Before, I presumed to be living with an animal and chalked up her civilised behavior to domestication. Each new day at her side, each hour spent in observation, brought us closer together. What had once been cohabitation revealed itself to be companionship. I was compelled to think we shared a sort of domestic tranquillity. My senses became fine-tuned instruments. In truth, the scenario was transformed as if by magic once one ceased to view her as an animal. Yet she was one of them.

Eyes are designed to look, but few observe and even fewer truly see. Yet another night spent on the balcony, barely protected from the falling snow. Before, I would have been blind to mountains of marble; but by then I was able to distinguish grains of sand on the horizon. The beasts were testing the mettle of our straggling defences in a minor skirmish. Gruner injured a rather small monster. Four others came to his aid. Oh my Lord. What we had seen as cannibalistic furor was actually a struggle to save brothers-in-arms from enemy fire. I had found their cannibalism, that fever to devour flesh without even waiting for death, particularly horrifying. How many of our bullets had struck souls who were simply trying to save their companions?

# 12

Who was she? Countless times at the lighthouse I asked myself this same question, both before possessing the mascot and after my lust was spent. When our battles had yet to begin, and when the guns fell silent. At sunrise and sunset. I pondered the enigma with the weary lapping of each wave. The view from the balcony was a vast expanse of ocean, which we had always believed to be empty. I stretched the bounds of my imagination, asking her: Who are you? What are you doing here?

I would never know the slightest thing about her. I was doomed to primordial ignorance. She belonged to a race of beings that dwelled in the depths of the ocean. My fancy could not begin to fathom the particulars of her daily life, the principles she lived by. How could I ever know what had driven the beast away from her kind? I would never discover what had led the beast to find refuge in the lighthouse. It was just as unlikely that she could conceive of the motives behind my self-imposed exile.

I treated her with more tenderness than ever before. My first possession of the beast had been a desperate and fortuitous act. Her odour repelled me before I touched that skin. The feel and colour of such hairless skin, forever moist. It was hard to believe I had once felt such disgust. I was incapable of controlling my ardour. I must admit, the added attentions were quite deliberate at first. I thought that by being affectionate and making love to her as I would any other woman, we might grow closer. If the beast had any sensibility at all, she would certainly grasp the vast difference between Gruner and me. I hoped this would draw out her humanity, like a butterfly out of its cocoon. That was not how it happened. Against my will, I felt an ever-growing passion for her. But the beast remained unmoved. I noted a new love welling up from within, a love being invented by the lighthouse. But the closer I got, the more she resisted this unprecedented attachment. The beast never looked me in the eye before making love. Afterwards, she rejected every smile and caress. The beast regulated her pleasure as punctually as a clock striking the hours. And as coldly.

Although the beast tolerated my body outside of the lighthouse, inside those walls I became a spectre. She shrank from me. All attempts to attract her attention were fruitless. Gruner himself was an extenuating factor. I liked to think of her as private property, a being subjugated to my very intimate tyranny. But in the confines of the lighthouse she became the same witless creature as ever. Her master and his guns transformed the creature into something between a meek dog and an evasive cat. Any shreds of humanity I had glimpsed outside vanished like a mirage.

On those days, I no longer knew what to think. Perhaps I only sought to justify my desire. Perhaps I wished to make her my equal so as not to perish like a savage. On the other hand, I had renounced the world, and humankind along with it. I began to realise, while scarcely crediting it, that she was the refuge I had sought all along. The cruelties of the lighthouse disappeared just by looking at her or by touching that skin. I was appalled that it no longer mattered to me whether she was more or less human, more or less a woman. The good Lord did not rest on the seventh day. On the seventh day he created the little beast, and nestled her beneath the waves.

As it was, my actions were no longer linked to my reflections. I went to almost debauched lengths to possess her far from Gruner. Once, I brought her to the forest and we fell asleep on the moss afterward. That day, the disadvantages of such a grotesquely clandestine love were made patently clear. And that was not all.

My body felt like an unstrung puppet. Muscles were strained that I did not even know existed. I rolled on a bed of moss, my mind wandering through languid climes. As a little yawn escaped my lips, her hand clamped over my mouth like a fleshly sucker. My eyes opened. What was she doing?

I heard snatches of a coarse German ditty. Gruner's

boots were trampling the undergrowth nearby. He was collecting wood for our handiwork at the lighthouse. The axe struck pitilessly when he spotted an adequate victim. He groped each find self-importantly while laughing to himself. All I could discern from where we lay were his feet, four trees away. He drew a bit closer, close enough for us to be showered with shavings from the axe's blow. The mascot kept admirably calm. Unblinking, she held her breath and compelled me to do likewise. I obeyed.

Hours later, Gruner was met by a changed man. He entered the living quarters and sat down in front of me somewhat distractedly. I said nothing. He spoke of the same obsessions, the ammunition and damaged doors.

"Gruner," I broke in without moving, "they are not monsters."

"Pardon?"

There was a long pause before I repeated myself. "We are not battling fiends; I am sure of it."

"Friend, this lighthouse would make anyone go mad. Especially you. You are weak, friend, a very weak man. Not everyone is capable of withstanding the lighthouse."

But that was as far as I could go. Our differences had come to a crossroads. I shook my head, ever so tired. My reply came slowly; each word carried its own weight.

"No, Gruner, no. You are mistaken. It is not over yet. We must send them some gesture of goodwill."

"I cannot believe my ears."

"We must give them some sign. Perhaps then they will realise we seek a truce." Discouraged, I said, "Like as not, it is too late. But we have no other choice."

Naturally, I could not tell him everything. It was impossible to say that a fiend knows nothing of illicit love nor does it conceal adultery. I could not explain that his every argument was silenced by the hand which had covered my mouth in the forest. I continued my discourse until his fist smashed down on the table, scattering plates and cups. Gruner's pupils, blacker than ever, had narrowed to pinheads.

He got up from the table, not wanting to hear what I had to say. But there could be nothing more absurd than massacre. The enemy was not a beast, and that simple fact rendered me incapable of shooting them. What was the point of killing them? Why should we perish on a miserable Antarctic island? There was no reasonable answer. I held up my hands imploringly.

"Gruner, try to understand. They have a thousand grudges against us. Think of it this way: we are invaders. This is their land, the only land they have. And we have taken it over with a fortified garrison. Is that not enough reason to attack us?" I could not help losing control. "One cannot blame them for defending their island from invaders! I most certainly cannot!"

"Where were you this afternoon?"

The abrupt change in topic forced me to adopt a more submissive tone.

"I was taking a nap in the forest. Where did you expect me to be?"

"Yes, of course," he said absently. "A nap. Naps are always refreshing. Now prepare yourself, it is growing dark."

He offered me my Remington. I refused it, still cross from our argument. But he said nothing and neither did I. Unarmed, I blew on my fingers to warm them. Gruner took a handful of snow and threw it at my chest.

"Take that; perhaps snowballs shall ward them off."

"Hush."

She was singing. Steely cries rose up from the forest's black depths. The howls were long-drawn-out and tender. That tenderness racked us with horror. Gruner cocked his Remington with a telltale click.

"Hold your fire!"

"She is singing."

"No."

Gruner looked at me as though I were insane. I whispered, "She isn't singing. They are speaking. Listen."

We turned around. She was sitting on top of the table. Her voice soared out beyond the balcony doors. The cries outside seemed to answer her song. The lighthouse's beams revealed nothing more than snowflakes spiralling down from the sky. I entered the room. She hushed as I drew close to the table. The forest also fell silent.

That dialogue still echoed in my ears. My only certainty was that some phrases had been repeated more often than others. A word that more or less sounded like "Sitauca", and above all, "Aneris", or something of that sort. But any attempt to transcribe those tones was doomed to failure. It was an abandoned score. My vocal cords had as much in common with theirs as the bristles of a brush with a violin. Nevertheless, after summoning a large dose of imagination, I attempted a pathetic imitation:

"Aneris."

Our eyes met. That look was enough for me to venture, "Gruner, they call themselves Sitauca," in a very free interpretation of those sounds. "And her name is Aneris. They have a name, she has a name. The woman you make love to every night is called Aneris." My voice lowered as I concluded, "Her name is Aneris. A very pretty name, I might add."

Gruner had reduced them to an anonymous horde. I thought naming the creatures might alter his views about them. It made no difference if it was "Sitauca" or "Aneris." The practically invented words I formed were just a muddled reflection of the sounds they produced.

Gruner exploded. "You wish to speak the toads' language? Is that it? Well, here is their dictionary!" and he roughly tossed a Remington at me. The rifle spanned the distance between us. "Do you have any idea how little ammunition we have left? Do you? They are outside and we are here within. Leave the confines of the lighthouse and hand them the rifle. I should like to see how you do it. Yes. I'd like to see you converse with the toads!"

I said nothing, it would only have instigated him more.

He shook his fist. "Out, friend, you blasted milksop! Take up your post!"

I had never seen him in such a state before. Gruner was every bit as frenzied as if we were in the midst of one of the bloodiest battles on the balcony. He looked at me for an instant as if I were one of his hateful toads. I stared him down for a few moments. Then I decided to cut the conversation short. He was not listening. I left the room.

The rest of the evening was uneventful. Squinting through the peephole in the door, I spotted a few beasts dodging the beams. Gruner shot at them from up above, cursing in his German dialect. He was visibly agitated. Unnecessary purple flares blazed through the air. But what good would such a show of pyrotechnics do?

Gruner gradually grew ever more taciturn. He shunned my presence. When we were thrown together by the evening vigils, he spoke without really saying anything. Gruner prattled as never before. His words clogged our nights with chat, strangling all conversation so as to avoid the one topic worth discussing. I tried to show as much tolerance as possible. I needed to believe that, sooner or later, he would give way.

As I could by no means count on his help, I determined to take my own initiative. I would have liked him to have taken part in the endeavour. But he could not be coaxed over to my side. The irony is that it was Gruner himself who gave me the idea. During an argument, he mentioned the insane possibility of handing our rifles over to the Sitaucas. That is precisely what I did. We had long since run out of ammunition for Gruner's old shotgun; it had been rendered useless. A practical fellow like him would never regret its loss.

I headed toward the beach that had witnessed my arrival. From experience, I knew they often used the spot to come and go. I drove the shotgun deeply into the sand and surrounded it with a circle of hefty stones. It was a crude ploy, but it made my intentions known. Hopefully, my message would be understood. At any rate, we had nothing to lose.

Three more days dragged by and Gruner never tried to come between Aneris and me. Our coexistence, and the simple fact that I was better read, had made him consider me some sort of wayward librarian. Gruner shared the commonly held belief that books are a sort of antidote against the temptations of the flesh. He was convinced that we had no common ground.

It must have been most disconcerting to him that I never questioned his ownership of Aneris. I posed a far greater threat by suggesting that our enemies were not fiends. A brighter man would have considered this a most dangerous idea as it inevitably brought me closer to Aneris. Not him. Even Gruner's rudimentary logic should have succumbed under the weight of the evidence. Instead, the man broke down rather than accept the truth. Since he denied the entire theory, he was unable to face up to the particulars. His solution was to look the other way and feign ignorance.

In fact, Gruner was being besieged twice over. Now he was being attacked outside the lighthouse and in. It was not that Gruner was incapable of grasping reality. The question was whether, once inside the lighthouse, one felt obliged to find some meaning in the madness. He chose to mull away the nights and shun the days. He turned the adversaries into savages, transforming a conflict into barbarity, the antagonist into fiend. The paradox was that this reasoning could only be upheld thanks to his inconsistencies. All was utterly consumed by his struggle for survival. The enormity of our peril was such that all discussions were postponed, as if he considered them absurd. And once he was protected behind the barricade of his logic, any further aggression simply confirmed his views. His fear of the Sitauca was the man's one true ally. The closer the Sitauca got to the lighthouse, the more vindicated Gruner felt. And the harsher the attack, the less Gruner would reflect on his own depravity.

But I was under no obligation to follow suit. The lighthouse had spared me this last human liberty. And if it was proved that they were not in fact monsters, Gruner's world would implode with the force of all the arsenals in Europe. I was to come to that realisation later. At the time, I merely saw Gruner as obtuse.

# 13

It was a day like any other at the lighthouse. A grey-black tinge outlined the underbelly of the loosely billowing clouds. Thousands of them filled the sky like pebbles in a mosaic, swelling the firmament. An opaque sun radiated pale pink light behind this display. The double-barrelled shotgun had vanished, removed by unseen hands.

The Sitauca seemed less active the following nights. We did not see them. Yes, our intuition told us they were out there, whispering among themselves. But they scampered away when we lit the beams. Gruner did not fire a single bullet.

Was there some kind of connection between their relative quiet and the vanished shotgun? I could have mulled it over for a thousand years without coming to any conclusions. I could not be sure of anything.

I walked to the fountain, smoking all the while. Gruner was there, absorbed in another ridiculously useless task. As usual, his toil was a ploy to avoid thinking. It appeared as though he had slept in his clothes. I offered him a cigarette, out of goodwill. But I was in a foul mood. As he began to speak, I felt an urge to shout recriminations at him.

"An idea occurred to me," he said, speaking in the low voice of a conspirator devising an impossible scheme. "There is still dynamite left in the ship. Kill a thousand more and we would liquidate the problem."

It was as though we were two men drowning and he had told me to drink every drop of water in the ocean. The possibility of understanding the adversary was infinitely more attractive than engaging in an uncertain and criminal fight. Why should I take part in his private war? No, I was no longer willing to slaughter the Sitauca.

"Open your eyes, Gruner! They are defending their land, the only land they have. Who can blame them for it?"

"You deceive yourself, friend!" he replied with a raised fist. "You are only alive because I let you into the light-house. They will kill us if we do not kill them. Come back to the shipwreck with me."

After his speech, Gruner began to act as if I did not exist. He pretended to be alone there at the fountain, unable to hear what I said.

I carried on with my walk. It was raining and the drops sullied the snow. The ice on the trees was melting. One could hear tinkling cracks as the stalactites broke off. The path was clogged with mud. I had to leap over the worst bits. At first, the rain did not affect me at all. When my woollen cap got soaked, I simply took it off. But soon it was raining hard enough to put out my cigarette. The weather official's cottage was closer than the lighthouse and I decided to take shelter there. My old dwelling took me in like a beggar's palace. It was a gloomy day. I found half of a candle left behind and lit it. The flame trembled and threw dancing shadows across the ceiling.

I was smoking and thinking of nothing in particular when Aneris appeared. It was evident that he had beaten her. I sat the creature down on the floor next to me. "Why did he hit you?" I asked without expecting an answer. I would gladly have killed him in those moments. It was becoming increasingly clear that my passion for her equalled my disdain for such a man. Aneris was drenched. This accentuated her beauty, despite the bruises. She removed her clothing.

My descent into bestiality did nothing to alter the pleasure she gave me. We made love so often and with such intensity that yellow sparks appeared before my eyes. At one point, I could no longer distinguish where my body ended and where the cottage, the island or her body began. Afterwards, I stretched out on the floor with her cold breath against my neck. I roughly threw my cigarette aside and got dressed. My mind was taken up with trivial matters as I buckled my belt. I left the cottage. The cold air outside sent a shiver through my bones.

The drama unfolded barely one hundred yards from the lighthouse. I had decided, if only for a change of pace, to follow the north coast instead of taking the forest path. It was a tortuous route. The ocean was to my right; on the left was an impenetrable line of trees. Their exposed roots emerged from clumps of earth and debris brought in by the undertow. Often I had to leap from stone to stone so as not to topple into the waves. I was singing an anthem from my student days. And in the middle of the third stanza, I saw smoke on the horizon. It was a fine black line, which twisted in the wind before rising. A ship! Some mischance must have set it off course, bringing it close to the island. Yes, it was a ship! I stumbled haphazardly back to the lighthouse.

"Gruner! A ship!" And, almost without hesitating, "Come help me light the beams!"

Gruner was chopping wood. He surveyed the horizon with indifference.

"They shall not be able to see it," he pronounced. "It is too far away."

"Help me send an SOS!"

I hastened up the staircase. He followed unhurriedly. "It is too far," he repeated, "too far. They will not be able to see it." He was right. At that distance, the lighthouse's beams resembled the flickering of an insect trying to signal the moon with its fluttering. But my intense longing gave rise to optical illusions. For a fleeting instant, the vessel seemed to turn in our direction. That metallic speck seemed to become increasingly tangible. Of course I was mistaken. It slipped over the horizon's edge. For a while longer, one could still discern the trail of smoke, growing ever thinner. Then there was nothing.

Until the very last minute, I sent one frantic SOS after another. There were humans inside that ship, an entire multitude. Families, friends and lovers were no doubt waiting for them. Their final destinations must have seemed ever so distant. But what could they know of isolation? Of me? Of Gruner or Aneris? To them, this world, my prison, was nothing more than a distant outline, an insignificant and deserted blotch.

"They do not see it," Gruner said flatly, with neither glee nor bitterness in his voice. He simply gazed impassively in the direction of the ship, still gripping the axe and blinking like an owl.

"Look at you! You have not moved a muscle! Just what kind of man are you, Gruner? You won't help me with either the Sitauca or humans. Willingly or not, you have sabotaged every sensible plan of survival or escape. If castaways had unions, you would be the perfect scab!"

Gruner evaded me and made as if to leave the lighthouse. But I followed him down the stairs, hurling insults at his back. He pretended not to hear me and merely muttered abominations in some German dialect. I caught him by the sleeve. He pulled away; I snatched again at both his elbow and his shouldered rifle. We shot a stream of mutual accusations at each other. The sighting of the ship had burst the dam that had kept us from outright hostility. It was a long while before I realised that Gruner had grown silent.

Gruner's mouth hung open, mute. His head turned from side to side. The entire coast was swarming with tiny Sitauca. They were half submerged in the ocean or hidden between the rocks and water, like crabs. Their webbed hands and feet were almost transparent. A horsey snort burst forth from Gruner's nose. He stared up at the sky, the diaphanous light and finally the shadowy silhouettes sheltering themselves on the briny shore. He resembled a man lost in the desert who can no longer distinguish reality from a mirage. He took a step north. The little ones hid behind the stones. The majority were barely a yard high. The sight of those creatures was inevitably soothing. Even the tide seemed to crash with care, for fear of injuring them. They rode the water like a cushion while observing us with curiosity.

All of a sudden, Gruner's rifle was off his shoulder. He hastily fumbled with the lock.

"You won't do it, will you?"

Gruner swallowed a mouthful of spit. He saw there was no threat. They were children, mere children, who did not seek the cover of darkness to kill. And they had chosen that precise moment, just when the days were beginning to grow longer. Finally, Gruner decided to amble back to the lighthouse, distrustfully leaving me in his wake.

One bullet aimed at the sky would have scattered them.

But he did not shoot. Why not? If they were just irrational monsters, if we only owed them nothing but suffering and revenge, why did he not simply kill them? I do not think he himself understood the extent of his sacrifice. Or perhaps he did.

The little Sitauca, timid as sparrows and prudent as mice, pressed toward the heart of the island. In other words, the lighthouse. They did not dare to venture past the coastline those first days. The creatures made us feel like animals in a menagerie. Hundreds of eyes like large green apples scrutinised our every movement and spied on us for hours on end. We were unsure what would be the best attitude to adopt. Especially Gruner. A harmless enemy utterly confounded the man. This puzzlement brought to light his contradictory nature. Gruner's scruples set the limits of his stubbornness.

Gruner turned into a manner of human spider. He continued to scuttle out of the lighthouse at first light. The little creatures, fascinated, would begin to appear several hours later. He turned a blind eye, but swiftly confined himself to his quarters. Gruner often shut Aneris in with him, binding her ankle to a bed leg. However, he sometimes ignored her presence completely. His behaviour was more erratic than ever.

Gruner had a quite pungent body odour. It was another

one of his peculiarities. The sleeping quarters became deeply impregnated with his marked scent. No European nose has ever met with the likes of such a primal stench. The shutters were drawn to stave off imaginary dangers, throwing the space into darkness. I entered one fine day and detected his presence with my nose more than anything else. His murky shape was alongside a narrow window, keeping watch over the floating nursery the island had become. Light from the chink in the wall outlined his eye sockets like a carnival mask. It was not a bedroom, it was a cave.

"They are nothing more than children, Gruner. Children do not kill, they play," I said, half in and half out of the trapdoor. The fellow did not even glance in my direction. He put a finger to his lips in reply, demanding silence.

I also experienced a certain uneasiness. The creatures were otherworldly and inscrutable. They waged wars on us, only to send their children out onto the battlefield. Perhaps they considered us to be a sort of venereal disease, a malady only harmful to adults. Regardless, it did not take a genius to see the connection between the shotgun in the sand and the children's arrival. What sort of mentality was at work? Were they grand strategists or utterly irresponsible? How would they make their wishes known to us? Our rifles had always been thwarted by naked flesh. I had called for a truce with a useless weapon and they sent us a bevy of innocent bodies. Was this the most perverse or the most perfect logic of all?

The little ones quickly realised that I would cause them no harm. They began to step on dry land over the days that followed, while still keeping a distance. Although I did my best to appear serious, I often could not help smiling. The little ones observed me fixedly, doing nothing but stare and stare. Their disproportionately large eyes and open mouths seemed to be under the spell of a fairground hypnotist.

I penetrated deep into the forest one morning. A fur coat padded my shoulders, bulky trousers kept out the fallen snow, and I warmed my chest with crossed arms. It was not exactly a restful nap. My eyelashes batted open at the sound of a murmur close by.

There were approximately fifteen or twenty of them. They hung from the branches at varying heights, peering at me. The watchful state I was in made everything seem unreal. The trees were not their natural habitat and they clambered up them awkwardly. Their bodies were so fragile, so vulnerable, that I gave in to their curiosity. I feared they would be startled if I got up, and might get injured while running away. I rubbed the sleep from my eyes.

"Away with you," I said, striving not to raise my voice. "Go back to the water."

They made no move. I was encircled by a troop of midget spies. The majority were still and silent. Some whispered, while others wrestled one another in amicable dispute. None of them took their eyes off me. I could not resist touching the feet of the one closest by. He was seated on a thick branch, swinging his legs. The vegetation came alive with a collective giggle when my fingers grazed his foot.

It did not take long to gain their trust. So much so that the children became a genuine annoyance. Small bald-headed figures ranged all about me everywhere I went. They were just like the flocks of pigeons that throng the plazas of every great city. My waist was often hemmed in by a mass of heads. I would make a brusque gesture to shoo them away, but they only sidled a few paces back. The boldest creatures nipped at my knees and elbows, retreated only to charge again in a barrage of gooselike honking. All bedlam let loose if I ever attempted to sit down. Countless fingers fought over hanks of hair on my head, sideburns and chin. I slapped a few here and there. But I felt the sting of punishment more than they did.

In truth, I grew accustomed to their attentions in a matter of days. We sported about the lighthouse from morning till night. The only precaution I took was to always keep the lighthouse door fastened. The creatures would scrounge around otherwise. They crept inside as soon as the door was left open, taking the most diverse objects from the storeroom: candles, cups, pencils, paper, pipes, combs, axes and bottles. I once caught a little thief loaded down like an ant with an accordion twice his size. Another day it was a cartridge of dynamite. Who knows where they found it. I caught them, to my horror, playing a game quite similar to rugby using the cartridge as a ball. All the same, it would be unfair to brand them thieves. The concept of stealing meant nothing to them. The fact that an object existed was enough reason for them to appropriate it. They were indifferent to my scolding. They seemed to be saying that those things were there for the taking and belonged to no one. All my attempts at pedagogy, whether with feigned threats or affection, were useless. Shutting the door kept them out of the storeroom, but the exterior defences suffered for it. The cracks in the wall were resplendent with bottle shards in gaudy tones of yellow, green and red, mottled by salt water. The children yanked them out of the wall to fashion costume jewelry for their games. It was a black day when they discovered that the network of tins and string was an ideal toy. They dragged the clanking mass of rope and metal behind them while they ran. As everyone knows, children's crazes are even more contagious than adults'. I spent half the day repairing the damage. I roared like a dragon whenever I caught them being naughty. Since I was known to be harmless, they pulled their ears at me with two fingers.

I began to view the children as canaries in a coal mine. The Sitauca would never attack as long as their children were in our midst. I was more concerned about the young ones' safety than my own. I did not like to think how Gruner would react if the little band dared to open the trapdoor to his quarters. The most mischievous of them all had the look of an extremely unsightly triangle. A pair of broad shoulders angled sharply down to narrow, almost feminine thighs, as though nature had not yet determined the monster's gender. He could twist his face into a rogues' gallery of grotesque grimaces. The others would come near me only in packs, finding safety in numbers. Not him. The fellow often paced back and forth in front of me. He took firm steps, lifting up his elbows and knees with a martial petulance. I ignored him. He responded to my disdain by ranting directly in my ear. In those cases, the best thing was to take him by the shoulders and rotate his body 180 degrees. The little fellow retraced his steps, just like a windup toy. But on one occasion he went too far.

I was sitting on a rock as the sun was setting one day, trying to mend an already ragged jersey. The children had gone beneath the waves for the evening. All but the Triangle. He was the first to appear every morning and the last to leave at night. The little creature came up to me and began to bellow directly in my ear. I was not skilled with a needle and those strident cries were an added nuisance. Suddenly I realised he was clinging to me. Hands and feet circled my chest and waist. Not only that, he caught my ear in his mouth and began sucking on the lobe. He received a sharp whack of course.

My Lord, how the creature sobbed. The little Triangle darted about, crying and screeching horribly all the while. At first, I could not help laughing, but then regretted it immediately. One could easily see that this creature was different from the others. He ran tearfully toward the north coast, stopping short where the waves struck the sand. It was as if, all of a sudden, he remembered that no solace was to be found beneath those waves. Without a pause, he headed weeping toward the south shore. This time, the creature did not dare touch the tide. His tears were mixed with disconsolate shudders. The Triangle roamed as aimlessly as a spinning top.

Sometimes compassion takes us by surprise, like an unexpected vista through the trees. I asked myself if that submarine world was so very much different from ours; they must have fathers and mothers. The Triangle was proof that they also had orphans. Unable to stand his sobs, I threw the creature over my shoulder like a sack and brought him back to the rock. I carried on with my sewing. He latched onto my body once more and fell asleep while sucking on my ear. I pretended not to notice.

# 14

I knew that what appeared to be peace was actually a precarious truce, renewed every hour the guns and monsters were silent. But the Sitauca seemed further away as each day passed. I took great pains not to think about how they were sure to return, sooner or later. Wishful thinking is the most tenacious of human frailties.

The Antarctic winter was giving way to a savage spring. Every day the light shone a bit longer, stealing precious moments away from the darkness. The storms were no longer so brutal; the flakes fell less thickly. Sometimes it was hard to tell whether it rained or snowed. We were almost never hemmed in by fog. The clouds were much higher in the sky, but they were certainly not silent.

I refused to take part in Gruner's nightly vigils. There was no need. But I did not take anything for granted. The children's presence did not just call a truce; it gave both sides a much needed respite.

I told him, "We won't be attacked, Gruner. The children are our shield. They will not touch us, by night or day, as long as the little ones are with us. Rest."

He counted and polished his bullets.

"We can begin to worry the day the little ones fail to show up on the island. Perhaps something will happen then, I know not what."

Gruner opened his silk handkerchief, counted the bullets and knotted the fabric up again with care. He treated me as if I had never set foot inside the lighthouse.

Then there was the question of the Triangle. Once I let him near me, it was impossible to get rid of the creature. He slept with me every night, unaware of our anguish. The Triangle was a bundle of nerves, scampering under the blankets like a giant rat. It took him quite a while to calm down. He would finally fall asleep by sucking on my ear, clinging to me like an infant and breathing noisily though his nose like a clogged drain. But the creature was a blessing. The egotism of childhood put our suffering into perspective. While I was worrying about how to end that cosmic war, he was enjoying a warm bed.

Gruner sensed the perils of such an apparently harmless activity. We were playing, and that was all. But play, no matter how innocent, creates a sense of fellowship and equality. Borders cease to exist when people play together. There are no hierarchies, no past. The game is a space open to all. Naturally, Gruner felt threatened by something so simple and friendly.

Before he went inside, I threw a snowball at him, which smashed against his neck.

"Come now, Gruner, enjoy yourself a bit," I said. "Who knows, we might get out of this yet."

His glare branded me a traitor. Another snowball might have been one too many.


I had unwittingly, and without even trying, developed a routine. It was the start of a new day. After a bloody battle, the first rays of light divided the terrestrial and celestial realms in two. We had been given a shock at the last minute more than once. The island was practically devoid of life. There were no birds or insects. The wind and waves were the only sounds to accompany our own. Gruner and I dreaded calm weather. Smooth waters and a light breeze set our nerves on edge. We would set off flares at the slightest noise, convinced that the Sitauca were coming. But my outlook was changing. It took a great deal of effort to recall my past, a time when silence did not pose a threat. The island was bathed in light. Bands of little creatures gambolled around the lighthouse's walls. Gruner holed up in his fortress like an elephant cowed by mosquitoes. It was his way of turning his back on reality.

The Triangle had princely privileges. The mite hung from my neck and chest as he pleased. It was hard to believe.

I had kept the Sitauca out of the lighthouse for months with cannon fire. And yet, I was unable to disentangle myself from a creature which barely came up to my waist.

The Triangle had the hotheaded nature of impetuous youth. Throughout the day, he led hordes of young Sitauca all over the island. He dropped from exhaustion when the other children left, no matter how rough the terrain. I would find him curled up beneath a tree or rock crevice and carry him to my mattress. I do not know why I wrapped the creature in a blanket. The Sitauca seemed to be indifferent to the heat and cold. But I covered him nonetheless.

I fell into the habit of pausing at sunset on the very beach that once witnessed my arrival. The inlet softened the waves as they lapped toward the shore. Fireworks burst across the horizon as the sun lowered in the sky. Bolts of sulphur and swaths of springtime gold put on their show. Rays of orange and violet wrestled like flying serpents, twisting over and under each other. Those last flashes of light made me fall victim to a strange delusion. I wanted to believe that the Sitauca were speaking to me. Their murmurs, confused with the outgoing tide, seemed to be saying, no, not today, we shall not kill them today. At length, I would return to spend the night in the lighthouse.

The snow might have been melting, but my relations with Gruner were growing ever chillier. The weather was, curiously, the only thing uniting us at that point. Until then, we had been too preoccupied with the Sitauca to consider other, more fortuitous risks. A body being run through by a bayonet has no time to worry about a possible attack of appendicitis. The spring fell upon us with all of its Antarctic brutality. The tempests felt eternal with the Sitauca gone. Thunderclaps seemed to bombard us like heavy artillery. The walls shook. An unremitting light glowed through the windows. Lightning spread across the horizon, resembling a network of giant roots. My God, such lightning. We dared not confess it, but we were deathly afraid. Aneris was unmoved. Perhaps she did not understand the full extent of our peril. She did not know that the builders had neglected to install a lightning rod. We knew. Our flesh might be reduced to ash at any moment, like ants beneath some sadistic child's magnifying glass. And so, while Aneris kept her regal poise, Gruner and I bowed our heads and muttered incantations like prehistoric humans of old, impotent against the elements.

But this fellowship ended when the sky cleared. I had to conceal my emotions whenever Gruner took Aneris off to his quarters. Those nights were often sleepless. Gruner's hoarse cries resounded throughout the lighthouse as he pounded his slave. The man genuinely repulsed me. I could barely refrain from bounding up those stairs and snatching Aneris away from that greasy bed. On those days, I should have infinitely preferred to murder Gruner than any Sitauca.

He did not know it, but the most flammable charge of dynamite to be pulled from the Portuguese ship was me. My fuse was lit every night, and I knew not how many times it might be blown on before exploding. My passion for her had grown larger than the island itself.

I found the sweater she wore particularly offensive. It was an unravelling woollen rag filled with holes, which may have once been white but had long since mutated into a sickly greyish yellow. She freed herself of it when Gruner wasn't looking. Nudity was her natural state. Aneris moved with an admirable lack of modesty; the concept of shame was unknown to her. I never tired of gazing at her, taking in every angle: as she walked naked through the forest; as she sat with her legs crossed on the rocks; as she climbed the lighthouse steps; when she was as immobile as a salamander on the balcony. She lay with the forlorn sun on her face, chin up and eyes closed. I made love to her as often as I could. Although he abused her more than ever, one could never tell when he might throw her aside. She suffered through the night and was bored during the day. Our paths sometimes crossed. When Gruner had no other choice, he would gloomily trudge upstairs to gobble down some food. Aneris put our rooms in order while Gruner lurked about outside. She had a very peculiar relationship to objects. She considered shelves elusive and unstable. She insisted on placing our things on the floor. Our belongings were lined up closely together along the walls, each item weighted down by a stone.

On the days Gruner left Aneris alone, we would secrete ourselves in the woods. The little ones saw us together several times, and the truth is that they were quite indifferent to our passion. I tried to catch Aneris interacting with the children out of the corner of my eye. They had almost no contact. If anything, she treated them as an added nuisance. They might have been a line of communication between her and the others. The children could have brought messages and news. But they did not seem to interest her in the least. She ignored them just as we might ignore a colony of ants crawling about on the ground. One day I spied her scolding the Triangle. The little ones may have been troublesome, but he was more mischievous than the rest of them put together. She shooed him away, but he always came back, as though deaf to her shrill cries. I saw this as his finest quality. To Aneris, it was his greatest defect. But it was obvious that she was averse not so much to poor Triangle as to what the little fellow represented. I had renounced my people just as she had renounced hers. That was all. The only difference was that she was much closer to the Sitauca than I was to humans.

What was the use of asking unanswerable questions? I was alive. I should have been dead, but I was alive. They could have torn me limb from limb. By all rights, my cadaver should have been rotting at the bottom of the Atlantic. Instead, I was making boundless love to Aneris, beyond any taboo, beyond any law. And yet, it was impossible to get close to her.

Her reticence should not have surprised me, given her life at the lighthouse. Like it or not, Gruner and she were inextricably linked. In fact, I was implicated in his cruelty. On the other hand, she was clearly not being held against her will. Although Aneris did not appear to begrudge Gruner for his violent abuse, she did not appreciate his protectiveness either. It was as if that despicable man who possessed, denigrated and beat her was nothing more than a necessary evil.

A door opened within her after making love. I could see it in her face. She gazed at me as if through thick glass, with an intensity which might easily have been mistaken for affection. With all their limitations, these flashes of lust seemed to hint at some form of love. It was only a mirage. Asking for a caress was like pulling teeth. Her eyes glazed over whenever I began to speak with complicity of the two most solitary lovers on the planet. If I embraced her excessively, she withered.

But it is no good trying to describe a play without a script. Life at the lighthouse was ruled by the unexpected, and our story meandered along a far more sinuous route.

# 15

One day, the children did not keep their daily appointment. By midmorning it became clear they were not coming. The Triangle looked out to sea like a miniature buzzard. But his anguish was short-lived. He was soon clinging to my knee like a contortionist. That was his way of impatiently begging me to play.

I was the one who felt the children's disappearance most cruelly. They had been the only breath of air in a land charred by gunpowder. Aneris kept silent in her own peculiarly hermetic manner. Gruner was possessed by a giddy vitality. Although he refused to admit it, Gruner was aware that the Sitauca children had been sent to convey a message to us. Their disappearance meant that we would return to our old ways; that was all.

I observed him as he lined up the ammunition, constructed fresh barricades and fashioned new weaponry. He had cobbled together a launcher to fire off flares like projectiles from a row of empty tins. The bizarre object resembled a tube organ. Gruner was quite talkative, one could almost say jovial. The prospect of bombarding our assailants with the coloured flares cheered him enormously.

His efforts, however, were wrought from desperation. The war was already lost. Holding out until the last battle might justify Gruner's philosophy on life, but it could never save him.

We shared our midday meal.

"Perhaps they won't wait for nightfall," I said.

"Trust me. They are in for quite a surprise."

And, sticking out his teeth, he giggled like a rabbit.

Aneris was sitting with her legs crossed on the floor. Her body still, she gazed unseeingly ahead as if in a trance. I considered how our violence revolved around her as the planets orbit the sun. Gruner sank heavily onto the bed. His enormous belly swelled and deflated. Like Aneris, he was between sleep and waking. What was I doing with a rifle in my hand? I told myself that the weapon was a precautionary measure. Deep down, I knew I had no choice. Gruner opened his eyes. He did not blink.

He stared up at the ceiling without getting out of bed and said, "Did you shut the door carefully?"

I understood what Gruner was driving at. It was his way of admitting that the Sitauca might very well venture out in the light of day. His words could be taken another way. Throughout those days, he had turned a blind eye to the Triangle's constant presence. Where was the little one?

Gruner's concern was purely practical. He did not want the little beast meddling about during combat. But that Gruner should be the one to remind me of the Triangle was unpardonable.

I bounded down the stairs. He was not there. I was quivering with fear as I left the lighthouse. There he was, at the edge of the forest. The sun's lowering rays gave the snow a bluish tint. The Triangle had a finger in his mouth and laughed when he spotted me. There were several Sitauca on their knees behind him, holding the little fellow about the waist and whispering kindly in his ear. There were at least six or seven others in the surrounding undergrowth. I could only make out the glow of their phosphorous eyes and the outlines of their bald skulls.

A shiver ran through my bones. But it was not a trap. A plethora of webbed hands nudged the Triangle toward me. It began to rain. The drops fell heavily, leaving craters in the snow like tiny meteorites. The Triangle grasped my knees and laughed, demanding to be carried on my back. He only wanted for us to play together.

I suppose the Sitauca expected me to respond somehow to this gesture of goodwill. But then their muscles suddenly flinched. I looked behind me. Gruner had witnessed the scene. He turned about on the balcony, mocking yet anxious. He had tied his invention to one of the banisters.

"Gruner, they've come in peace!" I screamed, protecting

the Triangle with one hand and waving my other arm wildly through the air. "They mean us no harm!"

"Take shelter in the lighthouse, friend! I shall provide cover for you!"

He fiddled with the launcher. One wick connected each tin tube where the flares were hidden. The artefact was pointed directly at us.

"Don't do it, Gruner! Don't set them off!"

He did. The tubes were too short and the flares burst forth in every direction. Some sent a shower of sparks down on our heads while others hit the ground before exploding. The land blazed with fireworks of eight different colours. I threw myself to the ground, shielding the Triangle beneath my belly. In the midst of the confusion he slipped away like a wet fish.

The Sitauca leaped about, dodging Gruner's flares and bullets. The shots flew quite close to my head, buzzing by like a swarm of bees in my ear. The Triangle was caught in the middle and sobbing with fright. I was huddled over, gesturing for him to come to me. I longed to protect him. He hesitated. The little fellow knew not whether to take refuge with me or run toward the waves. It anguished me to watch this inner struggle. We seemed to be separated by a seamless pane of glass. Finally, he retreated a few paces. Then he went away for good. I could still see him bobbing in the waves. As irrational as it may seem, losing the

Triangle affected me much more than my failure to make peace with the Sitauca.

Once at the lighthouse, I charged up the stairs three at a time. I clutched Gruner's chest in a fit of rage, gripping him so tightly that one of his coat buttons came off in my hands.

"I saved your life!" he protested.

"You saved my life?" I bellowed. "Your pyrotechnics have dashed our one chance of survival."

I went out on the balcony. As one might expect, the Sitauca were gone. The Triangle was nowhere to be seen. It would soon be dark. Harsh gusts of wind blew the rain this way and that. Gruner's apparatus, nothing more than a heap of tin, clattered against the balcony's iron bars. The din merely exasperated me at first. However, I was soon sunk in a welter of fatalistic melancholy. What a wretched death knoll, I said to myself.

Gruner gazed fervently outside, repeating, "Where are they, where are they?"

All I could do was clutch my rifle. We kept close watch on each other, sometimes openly, sometimes on the sly. By nightfall, the situation became absurd. We were not speaking to each other, and yet we had taken up our posts, one on each side of that tiny balcony. I no longer knew whether we were keeping vigil over the surrounding darkness or just watching each other. Nothing transpired until midnight. The rain ravaged the snow. Streams of snowmelt cascaded down the rocks, sweeping up dead branches in their wake.

At one point, the moon shone through parted clouds. The gleam revealed a cluster of Sitauca. The beasts were at the forest's edge, in the same spot as before. They made no sign of coming any closer. I scanned the group in search of the Triangle. But Gruner immediately opened fire. The Sitauca dispersed under the rain of bullets. Some fled on their hands and knees.

"Look at your friends now!" Gruner intoned victoriously. "They skitter away like insects! Have you ever seen such miserable creatures?"

"This battlefield is no different from any other. I myself have crawled away when the bullets flew about me. Hold your fire! How shall we ever reach a truce if you insist on barraging them with lead? Hold your fire!"

I seized the barrel of his Remington with one hand and aimed it toward the sky. But Gruner brutally wrenched the weapon away from me and discharged another round of bullets.

"Don't shoot!" I exclaimed while reaching for his gun.

He reacted as though I had been trying to rend his arm from its socket. Gruner kicked me inside, his rifle poised in readiness. It was a declaration of outright aggression. He bellowed insults at me. I sank down into a chair and bit my lip, my face red with rage. There was no use trying to reason with a madman. He stepped into the room. Leaving aside the Remington, Gruner began to bellow out an incoherent and disjointed discourse. I merely looked on, my arms crossed like a defendant on trial. He waved the harpoon above his head, singing its praises. Aneris's skin had turned darker than ever as she sat on the floor, her back against the wall. She began to sing in a soft, reedy voice.

Gruner kicked her furiously with his foot, not attending to where the blows fell. In those moments, I was far more afraid of him than of the Sitauca. Furniture toppled over in Gruner's whirlwind of rage. He took Aneris by the neck. I thought he would snap it like a bottle. No. Gruner drew up closer to Aneris, whispering sweetly in her ear. He spoke in a completely different tone of voice than usual. And that was not all. Emotion screwed up his eyes in their sacs of swollen flesh. It would have taken very little for him to burst into tears. This man, coarseness personified, was about to cry. A book had fallen out of a toppled commode. It was the copy of *The Golden Bough*.

"My God, you knew it was there, did you not?" I intervened, dusting off the book's cover. "You have always known."

The Sitauca howled below, sounding rather more indignant than deadly. Gruner's entire body went rigid. Sensing the collapse was near, I kept silent. It was the surest manner to set forth the evidence, prove to him that he had not a leg to stand on.

Then, in a friendly and edifying tone, I suggested, "Gruner, all we have to do is offer them something in exchange for a ceasefire."

I believed him to be unmanned. But he pointed an ever more menacing finger at me. He reasoned with an ironic guile I should not have thought him capable of.

"Of course, you have lain with her. You bedded the beast. Now I understand!"

I had simply attempted to offer a reasonable solution, to parley for peace so we might save our lives. However, he had arrived at an accurate conclusion through false logic.

"Your amorous inclinations do not coincide with mine," I said in the most diplomatic tone I could muster.

"You have had your way with her! You have possessed her. I knew it, I knew it since the first day I laid eyes on you, since the first day you set foot in this lighthouse. I knew, sooner or later, you would stab me in the back."

Was he truly bothered that we were lovers? I doubt it. The accusation was just an excuse to vent his loathing. No, I was not guilty of adultery. I had committed a far graver abomination. My words had shattered his simplistic universe, uncluttered by nuance. That world had been dependent on a black-and-white absolutism to survive. It was fear, not hate, which caused him to beat me as if his rifle barrel were a truncheon. He feared that his toads might somehow resemble us, and was terrified of their making reasonable demands. Listening to them should oblige us to set down our weapons. That rifle expressed itself with more eloquence than any speech as it landed on my skull and ribs. Gruner, Gruner, had gone so far in his attempts to distance himself from the beasts that he had turned into the worst toad imaginable.

It remains a mystery to me how I managed to escape down the trapdoor. I reeled and tumbled down to the ground. Gruner followed behind, roaring like a gorilla. His fists pounded me with staggering velocity. They fell like hammer blows. Fortunately, my thick layers of clothing blunted the punches a bit. Unsatisfied with the thrashing, Gruner seized me by the collar with his two hands.

He battered my body against the wall again and again. It was only a matter of time before he smashed my skull or spinal column. His brutality reduced me to the level of a rat. My only hope was to tear out his eyes. And yet, as soon as Gruner sensed my fingers pawing his face, I was thrown to the ground. He set to booting me with his elephant-sized feet. Dragging myself away, I chanced to turn around and saw the axe poised in the air.

"Gruner, stop! You are no assassin!"

He was not listening. I went numb there, on the brink of death. Scenes from an old and inconsequential dream flitted through my mind's eye. Just as Gruner lifted the axe, an inexplicable thing happened. His features were lit up by a combined flash of debility and intelligence, like a meteorite coursing across the sky. He still held the weapon aloft with the doomed happiness of a scientist who has scorched his retinas in order to discover exactly how long the human eye can stare at the sun.

"Love, love," he said.

He lowered the axe in a gesture of sweet sadness. He resembled a father quietly closing the door on his sleeping children.

"Love, love," he repeated softly, a hint of a smile on his lips.

All at once, he reverted to his old savage self. But I no longer existed. He turned his back to me and opened the lighthouse door. I could hardly credit what was happening.

A Sitauca immediately tried to enter the lighthouse and was met with the axe chop that had been meant for me. Gruner snatched up a log with his other hand, grasping it like a club, and strode outside.

"Gruner!" I drew near the threshold. "Come back to the lighthouse!"

He ran along the rocks in a straight line. Then he leaped into the air, his arms outspread. For a moment, I had the impression that he was flying. The Sitauca assailed him from all sides. They emerged from the darkness, shrieking in murderously gleeful tones the likes of which I had never known. Several jumped on top of him and yet Gruner managed to slip away with one agile somersault. He soon became the centre of a wheel, keeping the Sitauca at bay by wielding the log and axe like little windmills. The clamour increased when a Sitauca leaped onto his back. Gruner made a woeful attempt at maiming the beast. He lost vital seconds in doing so and the circle tightened. Gruner kept the beasts at bay by striking the air, oblivious to the wounds the monster around his neck was inflicting on him. They would show no mercy.

There was no more time to waste. I climbed the stairs, one hand on the railing and the other clutching at my side, which pained me cruelly from the blows. A rifle lay nearby. I went out onto the balcony with the weapon in my hands. They were gone. Neither Gruner nor a single Sitauca was in sight. Only a glacial wind broke the utter silence.

"Gruner!" I stubbornly called into the void. "Gruner, Gruner!"

He was not there; nor would he ever come back.

# 16

I s it possible to mourn someone you despised? Gruner's character had been radically at odds with my own. But he was perhaps the last man I would ever see. Now that he was gone, I appreciated his stony impassivity and companionship in battle. My grief was a terrible weight. I was agitated and out of sorts. Death merged with daily experience. I spoke to Gruner out loud while attending to repairs or patching the breaches in my defences as best I could. It was as though I still had to put up with his rough voice, coarse manners and evening cries of *"Zum Leuchtturm!"* I often sought him out to plan a night watch or devise a new defence and was met with empty air.

I was subjected to a species of paralysis for untold days or weeks. It was a seizing up of the mind, not the body. I suppose I kept moving out of pure inertia. Gruner was dead and I had lost all will to continue. Two men in the face of adversity are an army; Gruner and I had provided ample proof of that. A lone soul is worth almost nothing. I had pinned all my hopes on negotiating with the enemy. However, Gruner's suicide sabotaged the very foundation of my strategy. Of what use would peace be to them now, when I might be slaughtered with impunity? They would certainly have no wish to negotiate after Gruner's last bombardment. I had almost no ammunition left. My arsenal had been reduced by half. Just a few more battles and the lighthouse would be in ruins. I was alone and practically defenceless.

That is why the Sitauca's behavior so terrified me. Gruner's death was met with silence. They made no forays onto the island. I could hardly give credit to those incredibly placid waves. The nights plodded along without incident. I would sit on the balcony, my rifle leaning against the railing, while Aneris stayed thankfully mute. I felt like an emptied-out bottle by the first glimmerings of dawn.

I distanced myself from Aneris throughout those days of solitary mourning. I did not lay a hand on her, even though we slept side by side in Gruner's bed. Her distant and cold demeanour only deepened my lonely desolation. It oppressed me to see her act as if nothing had happened. Aneris collected and stacked firewood, filled baskets and lugged them inside. She would contemplate the sunset, sleep, wake up. Her range of activities was restricted to the most basic operations. Aneris's daily life was made up of a series of repetitive movements, like a machine worker trapped in the maddening confines of a factory shift.

One morning, I was awoken by an unfamiliar sound. Not

yet up, I noticed Aneris kneeling on top of the table. She was playing with Gruner's wooden clog. The game was at once simple and irritating. She held the shoe aloft in her raised hand and dropped it. It banged against the wooden table with a heavy thud. She never could grow accustomed to our atmosphere, infinitely lighter in density than her own.

A nebulous cloud of thoughts formed in my mind as I observed her. She took on a malevolent stature. The problem lay not so much in what she did do as in what she did not. Aneris, ever impassive, had reacted to Gruner's death with neither happiness nor sorrow. How did she perceive the world?

It did not take a clairvoyant to see how, just as she had turned her back on Gruner, she would do the same to me. I had thought of Gruner's tyranny as a kind of human shell enveloping Aneris. But when the shell broke, there was nothing inside. It was impossible to tell whether her experience of life in the lighthouse was in any way similar to mine. I wondered whether Aneris was pleased by our conflict. Perhaps she even found it flattering to be fought over.

I tossed the clog out over the balcony railings and cupped her cheeks tightly in my hands. The gesture was at once an imprisonment and a caress. I longed for her to look at me. Perhaps then she would see an honest and humble man, without ambitions. A man who only wished to find a place where one might live in peace, far from cruelty and the cruel inhabitants of civilisation. Neither of us had chosen the cold and scorched conditions of that horrid island. Nevertheless, it was our homeland, like it or not. Our task was to make it livable.

It is hard to tell when my violent caresses turned to punches. My fury blurred the paper-thin distinction between insult and injury. She fought back. Her webbed hands fell on my face like a damp towel. My blows were driven by impotence, not hate. The last shove threw her onto the mattress. There she was, coiled like a cat.

I gave up. Why bother? What did I gain by beating her? Aneris's indifference and disdain told me that I would never be of any great importance to her. It was finally clear what a great chasm there was between us. I had found refuge in her, whereas she had found refuge in the lighthouse. Never before had two such contradictory lives been so close and yet so incompatible. But did such knowledge cool my desire or lessen my need? No, unfortunately not. She had the same effect on my love as the volcano at Pompeii, destroying all in its wake while preserving the ancient city for all time.

At the very least, the tumultuous scene had the virtue of clearing my head. For the first time since Gruner's death, I was not dogged by inner torment. My footsteps carried me beyond the confines of the lighthouse. The simple act of breathing fresh air revived me considerably. The salutary effect flushed my cheeks. I could tell without looking that they had taken on rosy tones. It took me quite some time to realise I was being observed.

Once again, they were at the forest's edge. There were at least six, seven or eight of them. It was the perfect opportunity to hunt me down, but they did not. I surrendered in the face of such mercy. Despite Gruner breaking the truce, despite all our treachery, I was being given one last chance.

Life at the lighthouse followed no set logic. One might think that I strode toward them, content to finally put into practice my scheme of negotiation. And so I did, but this was not the only motivating factor. As soon as I saw them, my every hope was set on finding the Triangle. I held up my empty hands and headed toward the forest at a calm yet deliberate pace.

What must they be thinking? Their eyes were bright with inquisitiveness. One could detect in the adults a bit of their children's sharp interest. Some looked me in the eye; others focused on my hands. Their every blink could be interpreted in a thousand different ways. I considered how our mutual curiosity might serve as a potent antidote against violence.

But the lighthouse was the realm of fear. I was invaded by doubt as if a hornet had crawled, suddenly and painfully, into my ear. I began to question myself. Soon my internal dialogue became more convincing than the Sitauca. What if they were fighting for something besides the island? After all, what would they want with such a desolate land, with its absurd vegetation and jagged rocks? Perhaps, just perhaps, they sought something far more precious: exactly that which I desired.

I realised that the Sitauca's attentions were no longer focused solely on me. I turned around. Aneris was behind me, on the balcony. The Sitauca were staring at her, not me. Aneris's tension was palpable. She gripped the railing tightly, a helpless spectator. Perhaps she did not trust the strength of our bond and feared I might hand her over to the Sitauca. Of course it was not so.

The mere possibility of their demanding Aneris weakened my resolve. The closer I got to the Sitauca, the more difficult it became to continue. My feet slackened of their own accord. The snow fell silently.

The sun soared above us, a small golden disk behind the clouds. I was quite close to the forest, to them. A thick root twisted in and out of the earth like a great snake. One of my boots tripped over it. Farther ahead, several Sitauca tripped over the exact same root. We had never been so close to each other.

I stood stock-still for quite some time. The Sitauca remained motionless. What were they waiting for? Did they expect me to offer up Aneris? All they could want from me was the only thing that I refused to give. Whatever their quarrel with Aneris was, I would never be able to resolve it. I should have liked to tell them even my life was negotiable. But a life without Aneris was out of the question. I could live forevermore without love, if need be, but I could not live without Aneris. What was to be my fate if I lost her? I loved her as a castaway loves life: desperately. I was miserable on discovering that knowing the truth does not change one's life.

The rest of the day was spent putting the living quarters to rights. The quarrel with Aneris had left it in a shambles. I tidied it as best I could. Aneris was not with me. She had disappeared soon after I returned to the lighthouse. She would come back.

Aneris, fearfully timid, opened the trapdoor just before nightfall. If she had expected a violent reception, she was mistaken. I ignored her. I continued about my tasks with the hammer and saw her for no little while. Then I sat down at the mended table, smoking and drinking gin as if no one else were about. Aneris had found refuge behind the iron stove. I could see her in profile: knees, feet and hands clasped around her legs. Every now and then she would turn her head to spy on me.

I had finished another bottle. Our supply of spirits was stored in a large chest converted into a liquor cabinet on the top floor, next to the beacon. Despite the constant threat of attack, I did not mind getting drunk. However, I had second thoughts on my way to the stairs. Taking hold of one foot, I dragged Aneris out from her hiding place. I forced her to stand up, only to knock her down with such a strong slap that my palm was still red the next morning. She lay curled up and crying on the ground.

My God, how I longed for her. But that night, adding insult to injury meant leaving her untouched.

# 17

I lay in a drunken stupor for three days and three nights. Or perhaps it was longer. I would occasionally try to take up my post on the balcony in the gathering darkness. All I managed to do was doze off. My fingers were tinged an ugly dark purple by morning. Touching the metal trigger was enough to practically amputate my index finger. I was alive because the Sitauca were planning their last assault with the utmost care. I owed my survival to a respect that had been pounded into the monsters with bullets. It was a poor consolation.

I found constant intoxication to hold far more advantages than inconveniences. Above all, I could sense that my desire for Aneris was weakening. I, too, clothed her in order to spare myself the spectacle of dazzling flesh. It was a black sweater, patched with ungainly scraps of sackcloth. The sleeves were too long for her arms, and the garment fell to her knees. I would now and again boot her smartly when she was within range, not bothering to move from my seat.

Nevertheless, all these self-important airs were useless. My taunts only served to underscore how little power I truly had. I was weaker than an empire defended by a bulwark of smoke, or an army of tin soldiers. Whenever I became too drunk or too sober, the artifice crumbled. She never put up any resistance. Why should she? The more I feigned an absolute control over Aneris, the more obvious my wretchedness grew. Our sex simply confirmed that I was living in a prison, with deserts of water and ice for bars. If only it had been pure lust that guided me. Often my own pleasure was cut short by a flood of pathetic tears.

On what would be the last morning of my binge, Aneris had the temerity to wake me. She tugged on one of my toes with all her strength and yet I hardly blinked. A familiar pain had settled in the back of my sinuses, the result of my excesses with gin. I breathed through sugar. Although barely conscious, I calculated that it was simpler to ignore her rather than fight back. But she persisted by pulling on my hair. Pain became muddled with rage. Still blinded by sleep, I attempted to strike her. She eluded me, making clicking noises like an agitated little telegraph. I threw one empty bottle, and then another, at her wavering form. Then Aneris skittered down through the trapdoor, leaving me to descend once again into a bitter and unpleasant stupor.

I was caught between sleeping and waking. How long did I remain in that pitiful state? Slowly, the confused haze cleared and I realised that Aneris must have had a very good reason to disturb such an irascible drunk.

Dawn touched the balcony with a timid intelligence, as if the sun had only just discovered the island. Suddenly I heard them. There were voices inside the lighthouse, on the floor below. A cacophony of sound rose up through the stairwell. My vocal cords had ceased to function. I strung words together like a moribund: rifle, rope, flare. I felt transfixed by an uncanny hypnosis, and could do nothing but stare at the trapdoor.

Those wooden planks began to rise. Then a captain's cap appeared, emblazoned with the insignia of the French Republic. I saw an arm, two gold bands on a cuff. This was followed by a pair of friendless, intolerant eyes, a long fleshy nose flanked by two drooping pink nostrils. A cigar was lodged in his mouth. The fellow did not pay any particular attention to my presence. He was almost entirely in the room when a bottle sticking out of his peacoat got caught in the door.

He dissimulated by bellowing, "Maritime Signaller, why didn't you answer me? What has happened on this devilish island?"

The captain's face was sullied by a sandpapery beard. A legion of rodents had gnawed away at his bluish jacket, as though the man had not touched port in years. The crew stank of barracks disinfectant. They were sailors from the colonies, mainly Asians or mulattos, each one a different shade. The men wore no uniform and looked like a band of mercenaries. Those fellows would never be able to conceive of how much their presence disturbed me. My senses were dulled by isolation. All at once I was being inundated by dozens of new faces, strident voices and forgotten smells. The crew began to ransack the dwelling without further ado. One young man stood out among the rest. He was not a sailor and was far better dressed than the others. His office clothes were ill suited for maritime life. A chain disappearing into his waistcoat pocket spoke of a watch hidden in its folds. The other men bore a mutinous look about them. This boy, on the other hand, had the sweet face of someone who has read one light novel too many. He had a persistent cough.

"With whom am I speaking? What is your rank?" the captain demanded. "Are you deaf, dumb, or ill? Do you not understand me? What languages do you speak? What is your name? Answer! Or have you gone mad? Of course; he is insane." He paused, sniffing the air. "Where does this stench come from? If fish could sweat, this is what it would smell like! The whole building reeks."

Some of the sailors snickered. They were laughing at me. Having discovered that there was very little to steal, the men turned their attention to me. The boy rifled through a sheaf of dog-eared official documents, saying:

"Before leaving Europe, I requested a copy of the international register of maritime postings from the ministry. A man by the name of Gruner is listed, Gruner." He looked up, doubtfully. "Or so it seems."

"Gruner? Maritime Signaller Gruner?" asked the captain.

"It seems so, but I cannot be sure," the boy admitted, adjusting his glasses. "It is the only name on the public record."

"Maritime Signaller Gruner," the captain said, "this man is here to replace the former weather official. However, we do not know of his whereabouts. If you are unable to offer us a satisfactory answer, we shall have no choice but to hold you responsible for his disappearance. Do you understand what you are being accused of? Answer, you brute, answer! The weather official's house is right next door. This is an island. You must have some idea of what happened to him! Do you think this voyage has been a pleasure cruise? The ship embarked from Indochina in the direction of Bordeaux, but the company obliged me to sail a thousand nautical miles off course to collect this man, just one man. And now he is nowhere to be found. Precisely on this island, the size of a postage stamp."

He glowered at me furiously, hoping that either his intimidating eyes or the prolonged silence would goad me into speech. Neither achieved the desired effect. His hand swatted the air, as if to admit defeat. A great deal of the captain's authority was based on how he handled his cigar. He exhaled a cloud of smoke thick enough to be chewed.

He turned to the boy. "Silence is its own sort of confession. I believe that the fellow is guilty and shall take him back to be hanged."

"Silence may also be a form of legitimate defence," the

young man said as he sifted though the pages of a book. "Do not forget, Captain, you were assigned this mission only after the ship that was to have brought me here in the first place got quarantined with typhus. We have arrived two months behind schedule. Who knows what toll the solitude took on the former weather official? Even if some misfortune has befallen him, this man here has the look of a witness, not a culprit."

The captain abruptly turned his attention to an Asian mariner who continued to rummage through the crates. Before the sailor knew it, the captain delivered three sharp blows to the scruff of his neck. The captain confiscated a silver cigarette case the man had stolen. He examined it severely, never taking the cigar from his lips, and then swiftly slipped the case into the depths of his peacoat. The youth was unfazed. He was surely accustomed to such scenes.

He held up *The Golden Bough* and said pompously, "Have you read nothing else in all this time? I must tell you that the world of letters has moved forward. Intellectuals today must appeal to higher principles."

No. He was mistaken. Nothing had changed. He would have done well to consider those filthy men who had invaded the lighthouse like clients piling into a brothel. While he spoke of summits of learning, they debased all they touched. He should have looked at me, who feared the noose much less than living among those men. I had chosen exile over chaos and would no longer be able to retrace my steps. He was hopelessly smug. If only there had been a scale in front of us, I would have challenged him to pile all his books on one side and Aneris on the other.

Naturally, the captain's threats were absurd. I was merely an obstacle and was treated as such. He tore off his cap at some point, bellowing all the while. He employed the headpiece as a lash, egging the men on in a mix of French and Chinese, or some such babble. Yet before I knew it, they were gone. I could still hear them on the stairs. Orders, curses and insults were bandied about in equal measure. A hush fell afterward. They went in the same manner they had come. The ocean was unusually rough. At times, as the waves slapped against the lighthouse, it sounded like someone crushing stone in a quarry. At other moments, the sea's clamour brought to mind a lion's roar. To have seen a ghost is not an uncommon thing, but I was under the impression of having been the first to witness an entire crowd. Or perhaps it was I who was the ghost.

I did not budge from the balcony the entire day, fascinated by my own curiosity. It had been so long since I had seen a group of men that their every move was a novelty. The crew set to repairing the weather official's house. They toiled most begrudgingly, goaded on by the strict orders of the captain. At times, the wind carried the clamour of banging tools and the captain's voice. But not even he put much spirit into the task. His taunting commands seemed overly theatrical. The captain struck a poor compromise between completing a mission and embarking as soon as possible. I saw a thin column of smoke rising, and the men moving to and fro. The captain began to drink more than he smoked. He paid little attention to the youth's suggestions. The captain took short nips from a hip flask, turning his back on the others for an extra swig. He was impatient to get away.

The dinghies abandoned the beach at twilight, and I felt absolutely nothing, not even homesickness. The ship seemed to sink into the horizon. Smoke rose up from the weather official's chimney. The trapdoor creaked open. I did not need to look round to know it was her. Who knew where she had been hiding.

I felt restored after eating a tin of baked beans. Aneris immediately obeyed when I clicked my tongue. She cleared the table and hastily threw off the ragged jersey. In her own way, she was content. I suppose that my drunken state had been both unexpected and puzzling. Yet there I was, faithful and not asking any more from her than she was willing to give. I, too, undressed. I was just pulling off my last jersey when she abruptly changed posture. Her face contorted into an electrified grimace. She sat, legs crossed, and began to sing in a melodious voice.

Blood began to course through my veins. I secured the barricades on the door, lit the lighthouse's beam and sorted what little ammunition remained. I wanted to keep a flare handy. My God, there were hardly any left. Was all in readiness? Yes and no. Everything was ready. My surroundings were so carefully ordered that they no longer needed me.

The Sitauca invaded from the east and west coasts of the island simultaneously. They had divided into two small groups, which then met in the forest to prepare the attack. They drew toward the lighthouse in leaps and bounds. The beam would occasionally illuminate a pair of eyes, which gleamed like greenish copper. While I was taking aim, an old manual of military tactics came to mind: a fortification should only be attacked by night and in superior numbers, especially in the case of insufficient arms. And they must always seek and find the enemy's point of weakest defence before initiating their assault. It may seem pure common sense, but true warriors are much in need of common sense.

They vanished, and a minute afterward I heard them howling on the other side of the island. The order of things no longer required my presence as I calmly cleaned my rifle and listened to the play of gunfire. I played dumb while another human fought for his life, there, on the same patch of ground. After all, what should I have done? Inform the captain that we were surrounded by a million sea monsters? Abandon the safety of the lighthouse in the middle of the night? I counted at least nine shots and all I could think of was that such a rash waste of ammunition ought to be prohibited.

I went to see him the next day. He was shrouded in a thick fog until I had practically reached the doorstep. As far as one could tell, he was more or less alive. Wild curls and swollen eyes. The man was still dressed like an insurance salesman. The island had never seen such an unlikely ensemble. I should have laughed, had I any sense of humor left. He wore a white waistcoat missing its buttons and a black suit, wrinkled in the course of battle. He even wore a tie, although it hung loosely off his neck. One of the lenses in his glasses had cracked into a spiderweb and his shoes were caked with mud. He had gone from being a petit bourgeois to an expatriated pariah overnight. A smoking revolver dangled in his right hand. Paradoxically, the diminutive weapon just added to his stamp of vulnerability. He trotted toward me through the mist.

"Mr Gruner, thank God! I feared I should never see a member of humankind again."

I did not reply; the man had been reduced to a walking phantasm. He followed me about like a dog as I rifled through the dwelling. A glimpse of the abyss provokes a sort of compulsive loquacity in some people. He prattled on and on. I paid little attention to what he said. Two crates of ammunition lay beneath two large sacks of beans. They were shaped like tiny coffins. A hush fell when I pried one open with an iron crowbar, as though we had desecrated a saint's tomb. I ran my fingers through the bullets.

"Oh, sir, I nearly forgot," he said, kneeling at my side. "There must be a rifle in one box or another. Weather officials are required by regulation to pack a minimal arsenal. I did not have my wits about me yesterday and somehow forgot to mention it. Luckily, I carried this revolver on board to fend off certain sailors' unwanted attentions. Who would have thought that I was to take up residence with the devil?"

"You never know where you may end up. We should look through your supplies," I declared.

"Well, you seem to have made good use of your supplies." Then he added in a meek voice, "Otherwise, you would have perished."

Although he was right, I could not help feeling vaguely offended. I could not tear my eyes, or fingers, from those copper bullets.

"Now you too must put them to good use. For my part, I have no qualms with splitting the island by halves. Take two boxes of ammunition. I'm sure you shan't mind if I keep one."

He blinked in incomprehension and stood up. The young man slammed the top of the crate shut with his foot. It was a near thing that he didn't smash my fingers.

"What do you mean by trying to take the ammunition to the lighthouse? It is I whom you must let into the lighthouse."

His tone of voice had changed. I observed him carefully

for the first time. He was the sort of man who meets his death with hope on his lips.

"It is impossible for you to understand. All is obscurity here."

"I have seen that much for myself: turbid depths, infested by skittering sharks."

"Indeed, you simply cannot understand."

I took him by the neck with one hand and dragged him to the beach. I was not the stronger of the two. However, he was disconcerted and my muscles were hardened by island life. I wrenched his head so it faced the water.

"Look!" I bellowed. "Last night was hell, wasn't it? Now, look carefully at the ocean. What do you see?"

The young man let out a whimper and collapsed onto the sand like a broken rag doll that had lost its stuffing and began to cry. Naturally, I could easily imagine what he had seen. If he had been capable of envisaging anything else, he would never have ended up on the island. A frigid wind lifted the fog. The sun was lower than I thought.

He stopped sobbing. "Nothing has made sense since I disembarked on this island. But the fact is I have no wish to die in this place." He made a fist. "No desire at all."

"Then leave," I replied. "That lighthouse is a mirage. There is no refuge to be found within its walls. Don't go inside. Leave; go home."

"Leave? How do you expect me to go anywhere?" He

spread out his arms. "Look around you. Do you see a single ship? We are at the end of the world."

"Do not trust the lighthouse," I insisted. "Only those who have lost their faith arrive on these shores. Faithless men cling to delusions. But one cannot embrace a delusion." My voice cracked. "If you had faith, you should be able to walk on water and go back from whence you came."

"You either mock me or you are demented."

"How can you treat me like a madman having passed a night in this place?" My bones ached. "I am weary."

I sat down on a rock. He looked at me in wonder. I had been a mere ventriloquist. The chains that bound me kept me from believing what I had just said. To my surprise, however, his eyes narrowed into lucid dots. He did not blink. The young man stood up savagely and took off his shoes. He roughly rolled up his trouser legs, setting aside his jacket and glasses.

Yes; the youth began to walk, without hesitation or doubt, toward the waves. I was taken by a sudden inspiration as I gazed at the boy's tender and determined back. He stopped at the imprecise border between land and sea. A wave, longer than the others, lapped at his feet. I shuddered from the cold along with him, as though we were united by some invisible cord. I was plagued by doubt. What if he left?

The rifle fell from my hands. I could not believe it. He

was actually walking on water. He took one step, and then another. The ocean supported his weight like a liquid bridge. He was leaving, abolishing the lighthouse and the evils that had kept the fires of war burning. He had realised that delusions are not to be argued with; they must be ignored. He had eradicated all the passions and perversions by renouncing them right from the start. That boy was the eyelids of the world. A few more steps and we would wake from our nightmare.

He turned indignantly toward me.

"What the devil am I doing?" he cried, with his arms flung wide open. "Do you think I am Jesus Christ?"

He turned back. By the time the youth had reached land, he had the spirit of a warrior. He was ready to fight to the death. The young man spoke of two-legged sharks, poisoning the water with arsenic, circling the coast with nets covered in broken mussel shells, which would cut like knives, and a thousand other deadly strategies. I went up to the water. A flat reef lay inches beneath its surface. So much for walking on water.

I sank down onto the beach, cradling the rifle like a baby. I let myself fall back until my spine felt the cushion of sand. Definitively, the world was a predictable place, lacking in novelty. I asked myself one of those questions to which one already knows the answer: Where had my little Triangle gone, where?

The sun was beginning to set.